Jack Carnegie

The Belsen Files

Copyright © 2022 by Jack Carnegie
The right of Jack Carnegie to be
identified as the author of this work
has been asserted in accordance with
the Copyright Designs and Patents Act 1988.
All rights reserved.
This book or any portion thereof may not
be reproduced or used in any manner
whatsoever without the express written
permission of the publisher.
This is a work of fiction.
Names, characters, places, organisations,
events and incidents are either
the products of the author's imagination
or are used fictitiously.
Any resemblance to actual persons, living or dead,
businesses, companies, events, or locales
is entirely coincidental.
Cover By Jack Carnegie

Thank you goes out to Paul Addy,
who has always shown me the greatest support, his eye for detail makes all the difference.
As an author he writes under the name Dan Wheatcroft and his books are engrossing, you just cannot put them down.

To Carol, my partner,
who helps me in all I do and to my best friend Max,
our black labrador who is in all of the books.
Sadly, we lost him on 8th November 2021 at the grand old labrador age of 124.He had a good life and was loved by all.
I miss him every day.

Books by
Jack Carnegie

The Sweet Water Tales
The Blink of an Eye
Into the Blue
The Way Home

The Sikora Files
The Auschwitz Protocol
The Architect
The Belsen Files

Chapter 1

Hugo Drexler

Ilse Gerver, known as 'The Bitch of Belsen' had given us a lot to work with. The files we'd uncovered in her loft had been invaluable to our investigations into historical war crimes committed by the Nazis and their willing accomplices. We'd been able to cross-reference them with our own, pinpointing names we could allocate to individual crimes we'd previously filed under our 'Unsolved War Crimes' archive.

My boss, Emil Janowitz, was a tenacious man, he'd been gifted a legacy left to him by a fellow inmate of Auschwitz, Aleksy Markowski, and began the quest to locate, arrest and denounce former war criminals from the Second World War. I'd taken the job he'd advertised, simply as a challenge to prove to myself I could do more with my talents as a New York cop, to actually do some serious investigative work.

The first case had gone well, I thought. We'd worked tirelessly to uncover the plot to pilfer Nazi spoils via the ratlines into South America and, once in position, the multi-millions were to be distributed to fund the planned Fourth Reich. Through due diligence, we'd uncovered the still active SS officer Hans Schröder who'd given the final order to kill all the remaining Jews of Europe in the concentration camps. Tracking him down hadn't been an easy task though, and what unfolded after we'd gotten our man wasn't the outcome we'd all anticipated.

A chance remark made on a neo-Nazi internet site had caused us to begin trying to establish the identity of a person referred to only as '*The Architect*'. Our theories developed but the final truth was difficult to accept.

Now, we had to move on, go back into the files and find the next assignment, it's how the job worked, it was all about taking one war criminal at a time, or as Emil put it, *getting a continuous solution.*

My colleague, Fin, had been looking into the mutual aid association for the former SS, known as HIAG, he'd become obsessed with Martin Bormann, the former private secretary of the Führer. After Hitler had killed himself in the Führerbunker in the April of 1945,

Bormann tried to evade the Red Army who'd surrounded the city.

On the 2nd of May, in an attempt to avoid capture, Bormann was believed to have committed suicide, his body supposedly buried nearby, but speculation continued surrounding the identification of the remains found in 1972. It was only many years later that DNA testing confirmed them to be his.

Fin didn't believe what he was reading about Bormann though, too many coincidences had been unearthed in the Schröder case, sightings were commonplace and his name kept coming up. Fin had also found a book written by a Nazi intelligence officer, Reinhard Gehlen, who claimed Bormann was a Soviet spy and had escaped to Moscow. At the time, conspiracy theories were commonplace, people wanted to see high ranking war criminals caught and brought to justice but I wasn't so sure of Fin's ideas.

He was good at his job though, he'd uncover a case if there was one there, I just wasn't seeing it at the time but gave him the benefit of doubt, he'd not let us down so far.

It happens sometimes, you fixate on a lead and find it difficult to let go. Emil had done the same, he'd latched onto an idea he couldn't let go of for a long time and he'd hoped our last case would give him the evidence needed to expose Hitler's right-hand man, Albert Speer, as knowing much more than he ever admitted, but it hadn't.

One day, Fin was talking out loud, not necessarily to anyone in particular. "Martin Bormann controlled the flow of information into the Nazi party and he was a close friend of the commandant of Auschwitz, Rudolf Höss. There's something not quite right, I can't put my finger on it but I know there's something to be found." I did the same thing myself, it was a way of reassuring yourself you were following the right path.

"I'm not so sure he's not a part of this, the ratlines and fleeing Nazis," Fin paused whilst thinking, "For all of this to have taken place, it couldn't have been just about Eichmann and a few members of the SS, all the millions of dollars stolen and the operation we uncovered on Kaspar Stahnke's computer, I don't think we're seeing the full picture here." He walked away and looked out of the window, deep in thought.

"Okay, what if Martin Bormann really did escape," he hypothesised. "The only conclusive evidence that his body was found in Berlin was by the Hitler Youth leader named Artur Axmann," he said, raising his glasses to his eyes and reading from a sheet of paper. "He reported that because the Soviets were closing in on him *'I didn't have the time to linger in my identification of the body'*. Coincidentally, Hans Baur, Hitler's personal pilot, was with Bormann when they broke out of the bunker, which is where I believe the theories first originated that Hitler and several other senior ranking members of the Nazi Party had escaped the ruins of Berlin. It's very possible Bormann and Stumpfegger died at Lehrter Station and were buried there, but something doesn't add up in all of this, there've been so many sightings of Bormann. Simon Wiesenthal believed he escaped to South America. I don't know what I'm looking for here but one thing's for sure, there's something amongst all of this, and I'm going to get to the bottom of it," he stated. I believed him, Fin was unwavering in his determination.

Emil commented, "I remember seeing something within the Sikora files, a transcript from the security log regarding the last few days of the existence of the bunker, it may shed some light on things, I'll pull it out for you, Mr Quinn,"

"Thanks, Emil, every little helps build a picture," Fin replied.

Somehow, I had a feeling we were about to unearth our next case file and was looking forward to it, the job was more than a paycheck to me, it gripped me with enthusiasm and there was an excitement about it all.

As soon as I met Emil Janowitz, I knew I'd made the right decision to leave the NYPD. There was something about him that just felt right, but the fact I'd later found I was a 'doppelgänger' of his brother, Filip, who'd died within the confines of Auschwitz, at first unnerved me a little. Later, I'd taken it as a compliment that he'd confided in me, providing me with an understanding of his sibling within our talks I'd have lacked otherwise, and I was happy he'd chosen me to do that with.

Fin began speaking slowly and quietly, thinking out loud again, "Okay, I think I've got a way in on this. Hans Baur was imprisoned in the USSR for ten years before being extradited to France in 1955. He recently died, I'm thinking maybe we can get some information from any surviving family members, maybe do a little investigative work, Eugene, it's what we're paid for anyway," he said.

I'd been looking at the notes we'd taken from Ilse Gerver's loft, checking a few things. I read about the liberation of Belsen by the British 11th Armoured Division in 1945. They'd found over 60,000 prisoners inside, starved and seriously ill, 13,000 lay dead around the camp, unburied. I learned about a nursing sister, Sarah Davies, who'd worked tirelessly to aid the emaciated bodies of the stricken survivors there, a real special person to do that kind of work, I thought, and a picture of her wearing a gas mask caught my eye, it must have helped disguise the stench of the rotting bodies. It was distressing to see the state the inmates had been left in and the conditions Sister Davies and her team worked under.

Whilst cross-referencing the Belsen files with the files we'd unearthed from the computer Fin had 'liberated' from Kaspar Stahnke upon his arrest, the name 'Hugo Drexler' came up but there was an odd link to his name in there as well, a cropped photograph of two men. Ordinarily, I wouldn't have taken much notice of something like that but this one was of Martin Bormann and another, older man, smiling warmly at each other.

We discovered Drexler was at Bergen Belsen when the British troops liberated the camp in the April of 1945 and, for all intents and purposes, he'd been just one of the Nazi guards ordered to bury the dead. A resourceful individual, he'd escaped his captors using the very clothes of the dead he'd been tasked to bury and extensive research into the war crime trials showed he'd never been indicted. He'd managed to evade the justice that would condemn some of his colleagues to the gallows. In the absence of any reports of his death, we naturally concluded he was alive and had probably sought the assistance of the network known as 'Die Spinne – The Spider'. He'd slipped the country and the threat of the noose.

Where he was now we didn't know but the obvious place to start was South America. Experience told us that's where most of these people headed, seeking the protection of sympathetic right-wing governments.

It was a mammoth task but Fin, on seeing the Bormann connection, had the bit between his teeth and, surprisingly, found a 'Hugo Drexler' by using telephone directories and multiple calls to the phone operators of several countries. He was in Paraguay, at least he had been, and relatively recently too. Fin called the number, claiming to be a salesman, and discovered from the grumpy new occupant that Drexler had moved on several years ago, giving the impression he was buying a new house.

"How'd you get this number?" they'd demanded, "it's not listed in the directory." Fin broke the news his name might not be but Drexler's still was and suggested he sort that out. So, Drexler hadn't even changed his name and seemingly hadn't a care in the world.

We needed to dig deeper to find out where he was and what he knew of Martin Bormann in the aftermath of the downfall of Berlin, but it would be Sister Davies who unexpectedly came to the forefront of my investigation. An examination of the archived medical records, made during the liberation period of Belsen, showed the surprising information that she had treated Drexler for wounds he'd sustained in the deliverance of the camp and was possibly the last person to see him before his escape. She'd now be in her late seventies. I contemplated my next move, her photograph sat before me. She may know things about Drexler, things the various trials had been denied and I thought maybe she'd recall something that could help with our investigation. From her military records, I found she'd lived in a village called Stodmarsh in the south of England; a few telephone calls later had turned up an address, a residential care home; a place they called 'Rose Cottage'. I spoke with a nursing manageress, Laura, who gave me a little knowledge about Sarah, apparently she was a fun-loving lady with high spirits who liked telling a tale or two, which was good news to me. I let her know what my call was about and asked if we could speak. Laura informed me that wouldn't be possible because Sarah had become somewhat deaf in her old age and wasn't best comfortable with the use of telephones, so with that in mind, I decided to pay her a visit, besides, I thought, England was a country I'd long wanted to visit, I could utilise a little vacation and kill two birds with one stone.

I informed Emil of my intentions and filled Fin in with the details, neither seemed overly captivated with my planned trip. Fin was deep into his research into Martin Bormann, his obsession for detail was laudable so I thought it best to leave him to it, not wanting to disturb his train of thought. Emil gave the go-ahead for the trip and offered to pay the air fare and accommodation, which was a bonus to me as I'd planned the trip as a vacation. Later, I'd book two flight tickets whilst Jody, my partner, sorted the accommodation.

We flew out of JFK at ten pm on the Friday, arriving seven hours later at Gatwick International Airport, London. The journey hadn't been as bad as we'd anticipated and we'd killed time filling in crossword puzzles and trying to catch a little sleep, but I could never sleep anywhere other than my own bed. Hiring a car at the airport, we headed to the Red Lion Inn, a public house in the village of Stodmarsh where Jody had booked us in for the week. We arrived before midday and met the owner, Robert, a man of good blood stock he'd told us but the black sheep of the family who'd been ostracised because of the dreaded drink; the irony of the situation was the legacy which we were now standing in. He was quite a character. Within a short while, Robert had gotten to know us, his friendly manner known around the village, it seemed, and I noticed the locals would barter produce for beers which I found a quaint idea, a box of carrots would earn you two ticks on the chalk board for use later that evening, it seemed old fashioned, but it was nice to see that such a system still worked. I asked him about the whereabouts of Rose Cottage and he told me it was just a short walk down the lane. I'd planned my visit to meet Sister Sarah early the next morning, allowing Jody and me a little time to settle into our accommodation.

"Are you visiting family," he asked.

"No, unfortunately, it's work, I'm visiting a lady named Sarah Davies," I replied.

"Old Sarah! She comes in here now and again when she can escape. They keep her under lock and key you know, it's a damn shame, she's a good old girl, and brave with it, saw some terrible things in the war did old Sarah, the bloody Germans have got a lot to answer for," Robert pronounced, whilst shaking his head in disgust.

The public house was atmospheric, the cask ale they served was something I'd not had the pleasure of before. I enjoyed several pints that evening over supper, noticing the locals returning to stake their claim on their hard-earned beers. We ate heartily that night, a house special of lamb chops, fillet steak, gammon, chicken breast and sausages with a side order of fries that came shortly after. I commented to Jody, "They wouldn't have been able to fit them on the plate anyway."

We slept well, waking early to the sound of the dawn chorus; birdsong which seemed to emanate from the farm at the back of the public house. Whilst shaving, I recalled being corrected by a local the previous night, "We call them 'pubs' in England you know," I took that as good old English American banter, I guess some

Brits still hadn't forgiven our GI's for taking their ladies.

At breakfast, Robert served us up what he called a 'Full English'. I got myself some eggs 'over easy' in addition to local sausages, bacon, beans, tomatoes, a thing I can only describe as toast fried in meat fat and something called 'black pudding'. I'd not heard of it before and asked Jody if she knew what it was. She smiled, told me it was delicious and said she'd tell me later. Accompanied by a ridiculous amount of toast and some pots of jam, I made a mental note to skip lunch and gave it my best shot, not wanting to offend, but even I had to concede defeat in the end.

Jody planned a country walk whilst I paid my visit to the rest home. "I need to walk some of this food off. Jeez," she laughed, whilst rubbing her stomach.

I took a cell call from Fin. "Hi, Eugene, when you go to see Sister Davies, ask her about an SS tattoo, specifically if she recalls Drexler having one. If he did, it means he was genuine SS, not just any old guard at Belsen and that's a game-changer in regards to how he escaped justice. He was thought to be a junior squad leader at Belsen, papers suggest he transferred in from another branch of the military and it wasn't common practice for such people to have had the tattoo, therefore he wouldn't have been considered a member of the Waffen SS. If the tattoo is confirmed by Davies, we have something. As a genuine SS Unterscharführer, he'd probably have been assigned the position of Blockführer, in charge of a prison barracks, this would distinguish him between the two roles of simple perimeter guard or active participant. As we know, the Waffen SS had their blood group tattooed on the underside of their left arm, so if he's got one, he's the genuine article and I reckon his escape was most definitely organised by the Die Spinne network."

We knew how big this organisation had grown after the war and weren't convinced, at all, that it had ceased to exist. It would be a dangerous entity, we couldn't afford to make a single mistake if Fin's assertions were true.

Minutes later, he called me back. "Remember we discussed the Nazi regeneration experiments a while back, specifically the 'Lazarus Project' that Stahnke was trying to 'sell' to us? I've been doing some serious research on that, including a lot of time at the main library. They knew about DNA, Eugene. The German-Swiss scientist Miescher discovered it in 1869, for crying out loud! We *know* from the last case, the SS medical department was keeping selected samples from when they were testing SS men's blood for grouping, so what reason would they do that? Maybe they wanted to raise the dead and replicate what they considered to be the greatest Nazi warriors or minds. *Maybe*, Stahnke wasn't just bullshitting after all?" Then he added, "The question remains, who would they resurrect? Bormann perhaps? There's got to be more." The line went dead, I guessed he was on a roll.

As I walked down the lane towards Rose Cottage, I thought about what he'd just told me, it was interesting if nothing else.

My introduction to Sarah was made by a carer who'd been informed of my visit. "Hello, Mr Kennedy, they tell me you're American, you've come a long way to visit me, I'm Sarah," she said.

"Yes, I'm from New York. I have to tell you, you're of great interest to me, Sarah. I'm hoping you can help me with a little information," I said, slowly and loudly in order to compensate for her deafness. "I work for a man who's been left a great legacy, a Mr Janowitz. He was an inmate at Auschwitz and a fellow prisoner left him a large sum of money to utilise in finding war criminals and bringing them to justice."

She smiled. "You can speak normally, Mr Kennedy. I found my hearing aid again, just this morning. How interesting, I was a nurse at Belsen you know, I helped tend to a lot of unfortunate people there."

"Yes, it's Belsen we're currently looking into, a colleague of mine has brought to light some new evidence and your testimony at the trials fits right in with it. I'm trying to find out about a man named Drexler."

Sarah looked at me curiously then said, "Hugo Drexler?"

I nodded. "You remember him?"

"Yes," she replied. "I treated him. He'd taken somewhat of a beating when the camp was liberated, he was nobody of importance, just a guard. I had the task of changing his dressings. I recall him vividly because."

She mused over something for a few moments then continued, "He was a good looking boy who didn't seem to be of the same sort as the other guards and I remember he was almost always in the company of another man, they stood out from the other guards, their uniforms were pristine clean compared with the others. Of course, then he escaped in a dead prisoner's clothing. I was told by an officer that four others attempting the escape were shot in the field outside the camp. Afterwards, I thought they must have been planning something for quite a while. A German bomber had distracted the camp's security by dropping incendiary devices and at the time we believed it to be gas."

I interrupted, "Yes, I've seen your photograph, the one in which you're wearing the gas mask."

"You probably thought I was wearing it because of the stench. No matter how hard you tried, you couldn't avoid the smell of decaying bodies, Mr Kennedy, and any success was only a very short respite." She paused. "I was told much later that he'd gone to Paraguay."

I was curious to know where Sarah had gotten that particular piece of information from. "Drexler?" She nodded.

"Do you recall who it was that told you about Paraguay, Sarah?"

"That's a good question, Mr Kennedy." She sat with her fingers against her temple, deep in thought.

I pressed on. "So, was it a British Officer who told you about Paraguay?"

"Yes, but I can't quite remember which one it was, there were several Intelligence Officers at the camp at the time. It was definitely Paraguay because I'd never heard of the place before so I asked him about it." As if for proof she added, "It's in South America, you know."

"That's what we heard too," I smiled, then changed my approach a little. "My colleague has asked me to query a tattoo Drexler may have had on the underside of his left arm."

Instantly, she offered, "He had his blood group tattooed on his arm, I don't recall which group, they all had them."

"All, Sarah?" I questioned.

"I mean the SS, they all had their blood groups tattooed on their arms didn't they," she reaffirmed.

"Well, that's not quite true, Sarah, and that's what we're looking into, you see Drexler's records suggest he was a junior officer and he'd transferred into Belsen from a non-SS unit, those men wouldn't have had the tattoo, it wasn't common practice you see. Your suggestion that he did have such a tattoo would tend to confirm his role at the camp was much more than the one he'd offered when first questioned upon his capture at Belsen."

We continued our conversation over a cup of tea and a tray of Crawford's biscuits, which Sarah told me were one of her little treats in life. She was a nice old lady, still showing a glint of mischief in her eyes and you could see she'd been a fine looking woman in her day.

We were talking of everyday things, her life, family and friends when she said, "I'm still trying to think of that Officer's name. I know that I know him, but it's just not coming to me at the moment."

"That's okay, Sarah, don't think too hard on it, I'll leave you a number and, if you remember, you can ask one of the nurses to give me a call. I know you're not too keen on telephones. I'm not the greatest of fans myself, which is why I chose to come pay you a visit," I told her.

I asked the nurse if it was possible to take Sarah out for a walk into the village, maybe buy her a pot of English tea and a cake, or something along those lines. I thought she'd earnt it, I thought it would be a nice change for her.

I rang Jody to find out where she was and we arranged to meet back at the pub. After the introductions, we all sat in the beer garden overlooking the village green, it was a beautiful sunny day, the rain from the previous night had brought all the flowers out and they were leaning towards the sunshine which bounced off the road that had been washed clean by a downpour in the night.

"Would you like a pot of tea, Sarah?" I asked.

"No, if you don't mind, I'll take a bottle of 'Mad Cat Pale Ale'. It's my favourite," came the answer.

I couldn't help but smile. "That's just fine. I think I'll try one of those myself."

We sat with our bottles of beer talking over Sarah's exploits in the war, she'd been quite a lady and you could tell the locals loved her, each one passing by asking after her.

"Hello, Sarah, how are you today? Are you well in yourself, my lovely?" a man with a brace of pheasant on his right arm enquired.

"I'm fine, young David. My, you've done well today," she replied.

Shortly after he entered the pub, a barmaid came out with three more bottles of Mad Cat. "They're from David," she told us. "Says you're a good old girl and you're to get it down your neck." Sarah smiled and waved at the man in the window who waved back.

We were enjoying the atmosphere and the views when, suddenly, Sarah said, "Captain Montgomery Roberts, that's his name. I knew I'd remember. He was a handsome looking man, we called him 'Monty' back then, He married a friend of mine, Deena, one of the auxiliary girls I worked with. I'm sorry it took me so long to remember. We exchanged letters for a long time, sort of like pen pals you could say. They lived in a little village in Wales, Rowen, I think it's called. It's where her sisters were evacuated to during the 'Blitz' in the war, she settled down there. They're probably still there." She sipped her pale ale with a look of satisfaction.

"Would that be a place we could easily drive to?" I enquired.

"Ooh it's a fair old journey I'd say, but a lovely place, worth the effort," she replied.

I looked at Jody who nodded in agreement to what she knew I was thinking. We took Sarah back to Rose Cottage, obtained her friend's details and said our farewells. I promised to write and keep her up to date with the progress of the case.

That night, I wrote my notes up, making a memo to order some flowers and chocolates to be delivered to Sarah. I also made the note 'Get Fin to research Paraguay, see what he can turn up about the ratlines in 45 and the photograph of Drexler and Bormann, it was cropped, I want to see the original, who else is on it?' A seed had been sewn in my head, it was the unknown German who seemed always at Drexler's side, curiosity had gotten the better of me.

Jody made a call to the number Sarah had given us and spoke to Captain Roberts, Deena's husband, who was pleasant and obliging. It seemed he enjoyed the company of people since his wife had passed away several months earlier and was looking forward to our visit. I felt sadness for Sarah, she hadn't known her friend had passed on, and I thought about telling her but decided against it, what she didn't know at the moment wouldn't hurt her. I'd break it to her later.

Driving on the left-hand side of the road took some getting used to but I adapted to it, I had to. En route, our journey took us toward Liverpool, the city where 'The Beatles' came from. I'd have liked to have taken a look at the place but we had something more pressing to do so we cut off shortly before, onto the main road heading towards Wales. It was a journey of around six hours when we stopped in a place called Conwy for some refreshments; only a few more miles to go to reach our destination.

The British called it 'the Blitz'; the Germans called it 'Blitzkrieg'. It stood for 'lightning war', the sustained campaign of aerial bombing on towns and cities by the Luftwaffe between 1940 and 1941. Children from all social classes were evacuated into the countryside for their own safety under a government initiative named 'Operation Pied Piper'. They were given name tags and a suitcase to identify them to their temporary parents at the other end of their journey and thinking of it made me recall a book written by children's author Michael Bond, all about a little bear from Peru named Paddington, so I regaled the story to Jody. "The author had apparently seen evacuees waiting for a train to take them out of the big city, scared young children who were evading Hitler's bombs and the author had come up with the idea that maybe Paddington would be feeling much the same and that's why he wore a label on his coat."

The countryside around Rowen was in all its full splendour, the fields were brimming with harvest and the meadows plush. I started thinking about the evacuees and how after the initial shock of being parted from their parents, they must have thought it a great big adventure coming to this place.

At 'Nant Cottage', we were greeted by Captain Roberts who invited us in. I was looking at a picture on a mantel piece above the fire, several evacuees all standing together when he said, pointing at the individual figures, "Oh that one is little Effie and this one is Annie, they're Deena's sisters, sadly all of them have gone to a better place now." He cleared his throat. "You must be thirsty after your journey, can I make you a drink?" he offered.

"That'd be nice, thank you," we both replied.

"Take a seat out on the terrace, you'll like the view out there," he said and disappeared into the kitchen as we sat down overlooking a stream that passed through the back of the property. It was idyllic, like a picture from a chocolate box. He kept a good garden, with plenty of colour and a small foot bridge crossing the creek, a scene which could have been painted by Monet.

"Shall I be Mother?" Captain Robert's said and we both looked a little curious at him.

He smiled. "I mean, shall I pour?"

As we sat enjoying the views and the tea, I turned the conversation towards Drexler. I hadn't exactly wanted to because we were enjoying ourselves so much but I had a job to do, after all Emil had paid the expenses so I felt duty-bound to get what I could from the situation.

"Hugo Drexler has come to our attention in the past couple of weeks and we believe he was a member of the SS, passing himself off as a subordinate. Sister Davies said you told her about the escape to Paraguay, can you tell me anything more on that, Captain?" I asked.

"Please, call me 'Monty'. Yes, that's very interesting. I was Intelligence Corps during the war and I was informed of an operation under investigation, code-named SPIDER, all about a German organisation called 'Die Spinne'. Our people at MI6 were looking into a number of prominent Nazis, from high to mid-ranking, from Martin Bormann to Klaus Barbie."

I let out an involuntary, "Barbie?"

"Oh yes, and many others. We found a lot of sensitive information within Belsen. MI6 believed certain personnel there were members of the Die Spinne network and it turned out to be true," he said.

"So you believe there were more than one SS within the network at Belsen?" I questioned, "Most certainly, I'd stake my reputation on it. I'd suggest several, some important and some not so. They all escaped via the ratlines to South America, the belief was the network worked alongside others. We knew of ODESSA and we suspected they worked on this one together. I believe their goal was not only to get their people out but also to establish the foundations of the Fourth Reich," he said.

"That's the actual page we're on, Monty," I replied and went on to tell him of our operation and the successes we'd had. In return, he gave me as much information as he could. The one thing that stood out was his knowledge of a Father Krunoslav Draganović and the ratline he'd helped create, which was how Klaus Barbie had escaped, the same route and contacts he believed Drexler would have followed.

Our journey had been worth the six-hour drive, I'd gotten a link and importantly the specific priest who'd assisted in the escapes of Nazis fleeing Europe.

Father Draganović would be an addition to the notes I'd send back to Emil, I'd unearthed a possibility to dig a little deeper. Captain Roberts memory had served him well. Driving away from Rowen, looking at the beauty that surrounded us both, I got to thinking how many high ranking SS had actually been at Belsen in 1945, and more importantly, why were they there?

Chapter 2

The Disciples

I kept thinking about 'The Lazarus Project'. Fin was right, there had to be a reason behind the blood samples. It played with my mind for a while. Having only recently seen the film 'The Boys from Brazil', I speculated if the storyline had been based on the same evidence we'd uncovered. I made a mental note to read the book.

On our return journey, Fin met us at the airport and filled me in on his updates.

"Eugene, we've got a case on our hands, I got looking through Stahnke's files again and there was something there bothering me. It looked like a system file but it didn't look right and I couldn't get into it. I got in touch with our FBI hacker friend, he said he'd been waiting for my call."

I interrupted, "Why? What did he know?"

Fin smiled, "He knew I'd copied the files and, after he'd broken the encryption, he'd suspected this particular file wasn't what it purported to be. It had its own cipher but he managed to break that as well. Just to rub salt in the wounds, he said he'd thought I'd have called him earlier. Anyway, with his guidance, I've been able to access that file and found a folder with twelve names inside. It was marked 'Jünger', one of the translations of which is 'disciples.' Here's where it gets interesting though, Hugo Drexler sits smack bang at the top of the list and there's another folder that has details of 350 million Swiss Francs, stolen from the victims of the Croatian Holocaust. Then there's another 200 Million being held by the Vatican, awaiting transportation to Spain and Argentina, all organised by a Priest, Krunoslav Draganović, who was sympathetic to the Croatian Revolutionary Movement. You might know them better as the *Ustaše*."

"I know about Draganović, Captain Montgomery Roberts told me about him," I responded.

"Well, the Ustaše murdered hundreds of thousands of Serbs, Jews and Romany people. In effect they were run as a puppet state of Nazi Germany. They ran their own extermination camps," he told me, then he reeled off a list of names from the file.

"Adolf Eichmann, Heydrich's 'bagman' on the 'Final Solution', he's the second name on the list, then comes 'The 'Butcher of Lyon' – Klaus Barbie, who worked for Eichmann and, *later*, the US Army's Counter Intelligence Corps. Known for personally torturing prisoners in the French resistance, his mission was to clear the Jews and Freemasons in Holland. Josef Mengele, the 'Angel of Death', who experimented on children in Auschwitz. Walter Rauff, who was responsible for the design and implementation of the mobile gas wagons that killed over 100,000 Jews and people with disabilities. He was an acquaintance of Reinhard Heydrich, they served together in the Navy and notably saw service in South America during 1924, maybe that's where they got the connections at the end of the war. Rauff served under Eichmann and Heydrich as an official of the Criminal Technical Institute of the Reich Security Main Office. After the war it's believed he was employed by the Israeli Secret Service. There's a lot of the people on this list worked for Western intelligence agencies after the war.

"Franz Stangl, worked on the euthanasia program, killing people with mental and physical disabilities. Kurt Blome, a high ranking Nazi scientist who worked in the field of biological warfare but used cancer research as a cover for it, he's another who worked on the Euthanasia programme, experimenting on humans but he was acquitted at the Nuremberg Doctors trials because of intervention by the United States. Some of my contacts in the CIA did a little digging on a reason why, it seems he worked on some ultra-secret programmes during the fifties and early sixties, which was all hush-hush at the time, but later it came out during the Church Committee meetings, back in '75.

"Karl Brandt, Hitler's escort doctor, a member of the inner circle at the Berghof, was convicted at a United States military tribunal and sentenced to death by hanging in '48, unfortunately for him he was of no particular use to the CIA." He gave me an ironic smile.

"Gerhard Bohne, who headed the systemic extermination of over 200,000 Germans with incurable diseases, mental illnesses and other handicaps in the pursuit of purifying the Aryan race. And of course you have Martin Bormann and let's not forget our man Drexler. Now, there are two other names in the file but they're not on the disciples list, *but* they tie in to all of this with strong comparisons. Maybe they just didn't make the final twelve for some reason, I don't know. The names are Horst Schumann, who was part of 'Tiergartenstraße 4', also known as the T4 Aktion; he was a doctor at Auschwitz who experimented on sterilisation and reproduction, and Ernst Grawitz, also a T4 member, who supplied the inmates to be experimented on." He paused.

"I've saved the best until last, the interesting part about our 'disciples' is Speer's one of them, plus one other, the twelfth member, but at this particular moment that person is unknown to us because the space for their name has been deliberately left blank."

I was astounded. "You've been busy, Fin, that's quite an interesting list," I commented.

"Eugene, most of these men are dead now, all bar Drexler, we have a golden opportunity to uncover and bring to justice one of the original 'disciples' of the devil himself," he said with conviction.

"Thanks for the ride, Fin," Jody remarked, catching him a little off guard as the car pulled up outside the Flat Iron building.

"I'm sorry for the dialogue, Jody, I had to get Gene up to scratch on the case," he said.

"It's alright, I understand, you've a job to do but let me have him to myself this evening," she remarked with a smile as I pulled the bags from the boot of the car.

I tossed and turned that night. What Fin had said got me thinking and I just couldn't settle; twelve men, most now dead, who collectively caused the death of millions of innocent people across Europe. The obvious thought ran through my head – was the twelfth man Adolf Hitler himself? The reality was it could have been any number of high ranking Nazi officials but it was then I understood what I had to do, concentrate all my efforts on Hugo Drexler and perhaps the twelfth 'man' would be revealed. There was no point in chasing the shadows of demons long since passed. I had to focus on him and him alone, he wouldn't be aware of the findings we'd made and that gave us an advantage.

I began to read the Belsen trial notes, thinking the more I read the more chance something would present itself to me; many of the guards had worked at both Auschwitz and Belsen.

I read that, in Auschwitz, female prisoners from the rollcall selections would be sent to Block 25 and once there, they'd wait days before they'd be taken to the gas chambers but they already knew their fate, the inhumanity shown toward those unfortunate victims was incomprehensible. There were so many despicable crimes committed between both camps, it was truly shocking. I came across the testimony of Irma Grese, who Fin had previously scrutinised, an associate of Ilse Gerver; she met Pierrepoint the hangman for her crimes. The slaughters, tortures and massacres were all very difficult to take on board, but it was clear both camps were factories of death, one way or another. The file notes I read were scanned copies of the originals, after many hours of struggle, I found a way to search within the document for individual names but unfortunately Drexler's didn't appear. I was disappointed, then just as I was about to turn the computer off and retire for the night, I thought I'd take one last look for the name on a search engine. What came up was an 'Anton Drexler', a German far right political agitator who, interestingly, was co-founder of the German Workers Party and the first Chairman of the Nazi Party, being succeeded by Hitler himself. I sat staring at the screen, could Hugo Drexler be related in some way? Or just another coincidence?

Waking early, I read all I could find about Anton Drexler, pulling information in from wherever I could. It appeared not much was known about his early life, his parents and siblings were unknown. Had I found something? Could Hugo Drexler be a brother or relative?

I took the train to Greenwich and met Emil, letting him know my suspicions as I typed into the database we'd combined. A photograph came up of Anton; he wore circular spectacles, the type almost standard for the time, and a moustache not too dissimilar to Hitler's. I immediately recognised him as the older man in the cropped photo from Stahnke's files. Then I searched for images of Hugo but located the cropped photograph we already had of Bormann and the man I now knew to be Anton Drexler. Why were these two connected? Add to that Hugo's name within the Belsen Files, the cropped photo in the same file and now a copy of the Bormann/Anton meeting here on a site with no explanations. Was there an *important* connection to be made?

"Did Fin find an uncropped version of this photograph, Emil?"

"No, he didn't have enough time, I'm afraid," he replied. "But we can try now, Eugene. First though, let me update you with what I've found. I mentioned a few days back that I'd discovered something, the last days in the bunker, do you recall?"

"Yeah sure, you said there was a security log."

"That's right. It covers a date, the 27th of April, when a Luftwaffe Pilot, General Major August Waldschmidt, entered the bunker to see Hitler. But, the interesting thing is, he was accompanied by another man, a Dr Lexer. Now, the high rank of the pilot signifies that Dr Lexer must have been somebody of great importance and I didn't need my little crossword solver to realise the letters were an anagram of Drexler. Coincidence? Maybe not, Eugene," he said.

"Now, you may be wondering what Drexler was doing in Hitler's bunker at such a time, which is understandable. I thought the same thing myself, but with a little more research I found that Dr Werner Haase, one of Hitler's personal physicians, was also present at the time, and I'm surmising Drexler may have been there to collect a sample of Adolf Hitler's blood. What if Drexler was working on the Lazarus Project as an overseer, moving from camp to camp, in a kind of SS advisory capacity, guiding the experiments in a direction that would benefit the project? You see, we've always believed that the SS had their blood groups tattooed onto them to assist any medical doctors in an emergency – any unnecessary delay in any transfusion and very valuable politically indoctrinated committed troops could be lost. But what if that wasn't the real reason. Have you never wondered why it wasn't tattooed on their chests? The act of a tattoo on the arm is rendered useless if the subject loses it. If they received an injury to their chest that obliterated a chest tattoo, well, they're good as dead anyway. No, there's got to be a bigger motive. If they *were* extracting a DNA sample, as we suspect, it makes more sense. What I think Mr Quinn is trying to ascertain is – what was the exact purpose of those samples?

"You told me that Sister Sarah said he was different to the other guards caught, did she mention his attire?" he asked. "Yes, she said that they had much cleaner uniforms than the others, and they stood out from the other guards because of it," I replied.

"That fits in with my line of thinking. You see, I reckon when the allies took Belsen, a number of SS officers who missed the opportunity to abandon the place probably adopted other uniforms to make it look like they were just simple guards and the reason why they wouldn't have been identified to the British was because most of the guys that stayed at their posts were recent replacements. So many of the long-standing regular camp staff had abandoned the camp that those left probably wouldn't have known who was who."

"I'm still trying to figure out why they were there in the first place."

He smiled at me. "Perhaps they were looking for something important. *Now*, let's see if we can find that photograph you mentioned."

Several hours and many cups of tea later, we found the full uncropped photograph on a website listed under 'Militaria'. On the right hand side of the screen, standing separately in profile, was a much younger man wearing SS uniform. It wasn't the best I'd utilised but it was enough to confirm my suspicions that the older and younger men were closely related. It was also clear that the younger had been a somewhat late addition to the family and the possible forty years between their ages made me suspect they hadn't shared the same mother.

Anton Drexler died in the February of 1942 from an illness brought on by his alcoholism, which was around the time Bormann was transcribing Hitler's famous monologues known as 'Table Talk'. The translations were based on two notebooks, one of which was written by Martin Bormann himself. I read with great interest Hitler's belief that science could never lie but religion often did and his wish for a unified Protestant Reich Church, amongst other things. I was looking for a link to Bormann but all I found was Hitler's ability to manipulate religion, to use it to suit his own needs at any given moment. Maybe this was why the Vatican would assist so many fleeing Nazi's after the war was all but lost, I thought.

I spoke with Emil, later that afternoon, something had caught my eye. It appeared Hugo Drexler was under Martin Bormann's command at one point, serving as a military assistant. Out of curiosity, I'd put their names into our own Sikora Files database, which returned nothing of significance, then I put both names into Ilse Gerver's Belsen file archive that we'd had digitally converted. It returned an SS blood group of AB positive but when I entered the names separately nothing solid returned and I was unable to determine which man's blood group it referred to. With that, I turned to the Simon Wiesenthal Centre who provided me with information that established the blood group didn't belong to Hitler's personal secretary; the natural conclusion being it must be Drexler's.

I now believed we had Hugo Drexler's blood group and a very good grounds to suspect he was the young SS man in the Bormann photo; I just didn't know what crimes he'd committed or how we'd use this information at the time but his name was in the Belsen Files and there had to be a good reason.

"Don't rely on the tattoo as a way of identifying Drexler," Fin said, the next morning. "It seems, near the end, SS physicians were handing out hydrogen peroxide tablets, which when wet would irritate the skin, the layers would simply peel off, and what remained was so 'bleached' as to be virtually invisible."

I had a blood group, AB positive, and a possible escape route via Austria and Germany so I thought it best to concentrate my efforts on that.

I discovered there was an Austrian Catholic Bishop, Alois Hudal, who'd aided Franz Stangl, the commanding officer of Treblinka and one of the twelve disciples on our list, and decided to focus my attention on that escape route.

Alois Hudal and Krunoslav Draganović had helped the fleeing Nazis and Fascists of Europe and the route I believed Stangl had taken was considered the second of two known converging passages. It went via Germany to Rome, then on to Genoa and eventually South America.

I discovered another Nazi, Erich Priebke, had used the same passage which gave me confidence I was probably looking at the same ratline Drexler may have used. Eichmann's name came up and also a common theme, most of these men were held in internment camps with fake identity papers at one time or other. I wondered if Fin's idea could be true, had Drexler removed his SS tattoo and falsified his identity, as Eichmann had. Alois Hudal would have provided them with phoney papers, ones that would help them gain a displaced persons passport from the Red Cross and from that came the international visa; the word of a Catholic Bishop being good enough for it to be rubber stamped. There was a route, one I believed I had to examine thoroughly or it would be like throwing a dart into a map of South America. My initial investigation started in Germany but then I found Hudal had used a stepping stone in Italy, known as 'Aunt Anna's Inn', located in Merano, northern Italy. Eichmann had used the same route to Genoa in 1950. Making notes, I tracked the paths used by Eichmann, Stangl and the other members of the disciples I'd identified. Not all Nazi's followed the same one though, Erich Priebke escaped from Rimini, Italy, and settled in Sterzing, a commune in South Tyrol, later he'd go on to Argentina where he lived in the foothills of the Andes for over fifty years until an ABC news team identified him and he was extradited back to Italy for a long awaited trial.

After weeks of hard work, I had before me three routes used to get out of Europe and into sympathetic countries that embraced National Socialist ideology. I chose to concentrate on the one used mainly by the 'Disciples', rationalising it would be the most likely for Drexler to have used.

Fin was still looking into Martin Bormann and updated me. "After the discovery of 'his body' in Berlin, the original Bormann medical reports published in '72 released only some of the information discovered under the microscope. Although the skull was identified as Bormann's, it was thought that dentistry performed on the mandible could only have been done in the 1950's, due to the technological advances since '45. Also, there were traces of red clay found attached to the skull, which was unusual, as Berlin's soil was predominantly pale yellow. When analysed, one of the places this red clay could be easily found was in Paraguay."

After a pause for that to sink in, he continued. "Simon Wiesenthal stated back in the sixties he believed, on good information, that Bormann was alive and living on the Chile-Argentine border using the name 'Ricardo Bauer'. Now, we touched on the subject of DNA in the last case, and I'm getting reports back that they've extracted a mitochondrial DNA sample from Bormann's jawbone *and*, if you remember, you asked Jody if you could copy a whole persons DNA into someone else's? She'd told you that under laboratory conditions it was possible to make a carbon copy of the host it was taken from."

"I do recall that," I replied. "So you're suggesting the skull of Martin Bormann identified in 1972 could have been a clone?"

"I'm just thinking out loud here, Eugene, just thinking out loud," he said, turning away to his computer.

"Maybe the jawbone wasn't Bormann's, maybe it was cloned or the DNA was transferred?" he said.

Later that night, I let Jody know what Fin had mentioned. She told me that cloning was now a reality and cited the Brits with 'Dolly the Sheep', an advance in science that had not long broken in the news. She said she wasn't aware of the ability to change the DNA in someone's skeletal remains. "So, it can't be done?" I asked.

"No, Eugene, that's not what I said. *I'm* not aware of it *but* in theory it could be done, I suppose."

I decided at that point not to involve myself with Fin's line of investigation, thinking it was a road I didn't need to travel. I had to focus on *my* objective; I believed Drexler was still alive and kicking somewhere within South America.

I was determined to follow Eichmann's original route out of Germany to his eventual capture but started the quest in Garibaldi Street, San Fernando, Argentina, the scene of his capture, believing that if I worked backwards I'd possibly hit a cross roads at some point and hopefully turn something up. The best way to do this was to actually be there, so I flew out to Argentina. Hopefully, I'd find a link – I didn't know how yet but I knew the skills I'd acquired as a detective would help me out.

Twenty kilometres outside of Buenos Aires lay the rundown neighbourhood of San Fernando, laden with blossoming jacaranda trees and rusting old pick-up trucks. I walked down Garibaldi Street, taking in its significance to history. It was a long walk, but eventually I stood outside a house where the man lived who'd asked the so called 'Jewish Question' and formulated an answer known as 'The Final Solution'. A chill ran down my spine. It was an eerie place where people passed by without a care in the world, but I knew I stood out, they could tell I wasn't from the neighbourhood. I kept myself to myself initially, the language barrier was a problem but I'd brought along a phrase book to assist me with that. I found a bar further down the street, where men played chess in the evenings. I bought a sandwich and a cola and sat watching, attempting to learn a few phrases to fit in. As

I observed the players from a distance, a man asked me, "Tu juegas ajedrez?"

I didn't understand. "Sorry, I'm American," I explained, gently waving my phrase book at him.

"Ahh, tourist? You play chess?" he said, following it with "You come for Eichmann?"

"Chess, yes I can play," I said.

"Good, you play me," he said sitting down opposite, holding his hand out towards me. "I am Juan Tauber. I speak English," he said as we shook hands. "I am the local pharmacist."

He spoke enough English that we were able to understand each other and converse as we played our game. His comment about Eichmann seemed forgotten as the game unfolded but he soon returned to it when I got the upper hand; I'd played chess at high school and knew a trick or two.

"So, this is a famous street, Eichmann is of interest to you?" Juan enquired.

"I wouldn't say Eichmann especially, Germans in general," I replied.

"Nazis you mean, there are a lot of them around here, unpleasant people," he replied. It was then I caught sight of Juan's profile. I hadn't noticed earlier and realised I'd come across the name Tauber before somewhere. Although his appearance was local, I was fairly sure he was from Jewish descent. After the game we parted company, I promised him the chance of a re-match the following evening, which he agreed to; we'd meet at seven.

I'd planned on staying for as long as it took to get the job done, to get the result I needed, but the reality was I knew that couldn't be. Eichmann's case had to offer me something quick, a path backwards in time was what I'd hoped for, some association of a kind. I realised others would have thought the same thing but there was just something eating away at me that wouldn't go away.

The following evening at precisely seven pm, Juan Tauber approached the table I was sat at. Like the previous night, he held his hand out for me to shake and greeted me with a smile that showed the whiteness of his teeth.

"All is well, Eugene?" he asked.

"Yes, it's been a good day," I replied. "I re-visited the place where Eichmann lived."

He motioned towards me with a finger to his lips. "Some of these old men knew him back then," he cautioned.

"Really? That's interesting. Do you know these men? Do they talk of their experiences?" I asked.

He looked at me scornfully. "Shall we play chess, Eugene? This is not the time or place to talk of such things," he warned.

"Yes, you're probably right," I agreed.

Whilst we played our game, I considered my next move, should I let Juan know the reason for my visit to San Fernando? Could I trust him? It was a gamble that could well backfire and leave me vulnerable, so I bided my time. Not wanting to offend my newly found friend, we played our game and I deliberately allowed him to win, but disguised it well.

"We should go for a walk now," he stood and motioned me to follow him. As we walked, he spoke. "You must be careful around here, many people still sympathise with the National Socialist ideals, it hasn't faded into history like in other countries, it still identifies within the culture. I must be extremely careful myself because of that, I like my legs where they are," he warned, then added, "You're here for something more than a holiday, aren't you? I can tell that, you have a policeman's enquiring nature about you. What is it you are investigating after all these years?" he probed.

I looked at him cautiously, wondering if I should trust him. "You're just a pharmacist, right," I said.

"I am, my family used to live on this street, back in the day there weren't so many houses, a lot less in fact. It was more like living in the country, but not quite as attractive. My father knew Eichmann to say hello to in passing as such, they'd exchange nods at the bus stop. He told me how Mossad took the man out of here. He heard, originally they wanted Mengele at the same time but had to abandon that idea as it risked losing Eichmann. They thought Mengele was in Buenos Aires but he'd moved on, him and some others," Juan told me.

I'd made my decision. "Alright, I'm going to level with you, Juan. I work for a man who privately funds operations into the capture and denouncement of former war criminals. I don't need to tell you, my work needs to be kept quiet."

"Who is it you are looking for?" he questioned,

"Does the name Drexler, Hugo Drexler, mean anything to you? Did your father tell you of a man with such a name?"

"My father is still very much alive, Eugene, maybe you should talk with him yourself? He only lives a few blocks away, but it's late now, he will already be preparing himself for his bed so we should go in the morning, maybe he can help you. I don't recall the name Drexler myself but if my father can help, I'm sure he will."

We parted but agreed to meet at 10am, when Juan would take me to his father's house. I pondered that night about Mengele and the 'some others' who may have left with him.

The next morning came and I was introduced to Juan's father, Héctor, a man whose looks disguised his son's origin, it was clear he took them from his mother's side of the family. "Is this your mother, Juan?" I asked holding a portrait of young dark haired woman that resembled Juan's features."

"Yes, this was taken in the sixties, my mother Eliana passed away several years ago, she was a very beautiful woman," he said.

"Yes, I can see that, she has very strong features like yourself."

Héctor interrupted our conversation. "Hugo Drexler! I've not heard his name in many years, 'the forgotten man' we called him."

I was surprised, after researching in depth about the 'Disciples', especially Drexler, here I was talking with a man who lived at the same time as the escapes to South America.

"You knew him?" I asked.

"We knew 'of' him. He'd had a small house built, not too far from here. Word soon got around. There was only one small bar out here then and people would walk a kilometre or two to use it. A few months after they took Eichmann, I was told he'd abandoned the place.

Maybe he thought they'd remember him." He had a little chuckle. "Yes, Eichmann and Mengele were the real targets, Drexler wasn't high up enough to waste valuable time on, or so I heard," he added. Gaining no further useful information, we posed for a souvenir photograph and I departed.

I made a telephone call back home, touching base with Emil about my findings. "I'm starting to think that Drexler may have escaped from Buenos Aires in the same company as Dr Mengele. I've information that leads me to believe that's possibly the case and we have Mengele's last known location before his death on record."

After the call, I lay on my bed, considering the possibilities, running through all I knew. Could Martin Bormann have had his DNA cloned to make it look like he'd died in 1945, or could they have replaced the jawbone to make it look like his, and if so why did they go to all that bother? Was it possible that the 12 disciples had planned the formation of the fourth Reich and, most intriguingly, *had* Hugo Drexler evaded capture for over fifty years and did he have access to the millions of Swiss francs plundered from the victims of the Holocaust? I couldn't sleep that night, ideas swam around my head, possibilities, probabilities and maybe's. I hadn't been instructed to work like that, so I had to try to be disciplined with myself and acquire proof to move forward. Although what Fin had told me was interesting, it sounded like a plot straight out of a Hollywood movie. I knew my line of investigation was correct and, if I continued along my own path, I was sure to unearth something of significance at some point, at least that was my hope. Fin was a hard man to ignore though, he'd surprise you with his findings, and you just couldn't ignore the flaws he'd discovered in the evidence put forward of Bormann's alleged demise.

He'd interviewed one of the doctors who'd participated in the DNA testing of the skull and he'd confirmed only a mitochondrial DNA sample had been taken. Bormann's children, therefore, could only be identified from their maternal line, possibly leaving the matter ambiguous unless they'd compared his sample with that of an aged relative with the same lineage. DNA profiling was a relatively new process, first used in the early part of the 1980s, and mistakes were common but that didn't necessarily mean things were suspicious, it just added to the mystery surrounding this particular case.

The question remained, if Bormann couldn't be identified beyond doubt by the mitochondrial DNA sample because mtDNA was only passed down through the maternal lineage, then how did they know who the sample from the skull was from? All our enquiries had shown the family line in that respect was long gone and no one was going to sanction exhumations not even if we located his mother's burial site. According to the records we found, only the SS held blood samples for their highest ranking officers and they most definitely weren't available for testing in 1972. Had Martin Bormann's death been covered up somehow, had he even died in 1945, and what was the reason behind it all? It was both intriguing and frustrating at the same time.

No matter how hard I tried to separate myself from Fin's work and attempt to concentrate on my own, he kept drawing me back in with curiosity, it was all highly suspicious at the very least. It gripped my powers of imagination, but it was a distraction that I didn't need at the time, I had to follow up what Héctor had told me. Once again I had to put Martin Bormann to one side.

Tauber had sewn the seed, it looked like Hugo Drexler escaped to South America with Dr Mengele or in his footsteps. I needed to get back home and find out all I could about the 'Angel of Death'.

I had a good feeling walking into Ministro Pistarini International Airport, I'd achieved what I'd set out to do, find some information that could push us forward in the investigation. Nothing comes quickly in these cases, it's all done at a snail's pace, patience is the most important thing to hold any value in, time would catch up with our man; short cuts weren't an option.

I got home after a long flight, somehow the trip had almost exhausted me so I took a couple of days off. Sitting in the apartment, overlooking Madison Square Park, I took in the enormity of what I was doing, not more than a year into the job and I'd been entrusted to follow a line of investigation into Josef Mengele's last moves in this world. It struck home how important our work was at that point. If I hadn't already thought it I did so at that moment.

Like most people of my generation, the name Mengele was synonymous with evil, his crimes went unpunished and there were plenty of them. He was a monster, undoubtedly the worst of them all, the man responsible for selections for the gas chambers upon arrival at Auschwitz, using inmates for human experimentation and known to enjoy his work. It was a shame Mossad had failed to find him all those years back, but because of that it gave me the opportunity to find the passage Hugo Drexler may have taken in his escape.

I now knew Mengele transferred to Gross-Rosen concentration camp in Lower Silesia just before the Red Army had liberated Auschwitz. Shortly after, he'd moved onto Žatec in Czechoslovakia, where he was captured by the Americans but not identified as a war criminal. It would be the SS tattoo that aided his masquerade; by not having one, he'd been overlooked as important. Eventually released, he obtained false papers under the name 'Fritz Ullman' and worked temporarily as a farmhand until the network of former SS members known as Die Spinne aided his escape via the ratline to Genoa. Whilst there, he acquired a passport from the Red Cross under another false name, 'Helmut Gregor' and sailed to Argentina. Mengele then married his widowed sister-in-law Martha whilst on holiday in Uruguay and obtained Paraguayan citizenship, which was where it got interesting. It was said family members and former colleagues were in attendance at the ceremony. Hiding now in plain sight, he'd used the name 'José Mengele'.

I located the registry office clerk who performed the ceremony, Ilse Bernatzky, her records showed he lived in Nueva Helvecia, Colonia, Uruguay at the time of the marriage.

Little by little I revealed the jigsaw, slowly piecing it together, hoping for one piece of the puzzle to expose Drexler. Weeks passed by and I seemed to be getting nowhere fast, I had a mountain of paperwork on my desk with all sorts of snippets about Mengele and his life after Auschwitz but nothing on Drexler. I began wondering if I'd followed the right paper trail, maybe he'd gone down another ratline with another 'disciple' or maybe he was dead after all. It was a period of great disheartenment to me, all the work I'd put in seemed to be accounting for nothing.

"It will come, Eugene, don't lose faith," Emil encouraged, but it wasn't looking good, something else was needed and I knew it, something had to jump off the page and present itself to me, but it wasn't happening at the time. I was at a dead end, not knowing my direction or even seeing what the work I'd put together meant, but deep inside I believed there had to be something, my gut instinct was telling me so. I was looking for direction, needing assistance but Fin was heavily into his research on Bormann, it wasn't fair to distract him away from that and Emil had left me to my own devices, he had faith in both of us and I felt I was letting him down if I sought his help.

Maybe a little time away from it all would help. I'd gotten too close, I wasn't seeing the wood for the trees, then just as I was about to take a few days away with Jody, Fin mentioned I should take a look into each individual member of the disciples. "See how many times they cross reference with Drexler, you never know, it may throw you a line," he'd flippantly mentioned. It couldn't be that simple, could it?

Chapter 3

The Unknown Nazi

A brief phone call to the Simon Wiesenthal Centre threw me off guard. I'd assumed that Hugo Drexler was known to them, the uncropped photograph showed he had high connections, but their assertion that he wasn't had shocked me. I realised that, all the way through my investigation, not only had I not mentioned his name to them but they hadn't done so to me either. All of a sudden things started to become a little clearer. Héctor Tauber called him *the forgotten man*. The photograph we held of Bormann and Anton Drexler had been deliberately doctored to eliminate Hugo Drexler and our own Belsen File notes were actually the only ones you could find mention of his name within, and even in those notes he was considered a subordinate officer. It was all so clean cut and clinical, the way he'd been written out of history suggested there had to be a reason, and it must have been a good one.

I jumped the train to Greenwich to inform Emil of my news, face to face. "I've overlooked the obvious, nobody, not a single person knows a member of the SS named Hugo Drexler. I've checked back through my notes and it's only the Belsen Files that have any mention of him, which is probably why Ilse Gerver hid them in her loft, why she said it was her 'piece of security' when she mentioned the files. She obviously knew they contained information that could protect her if needed. When I think about it, even Sister Sarah didn't mention Drexler in terms of an SS officer. When I spoke of him, she used the words *'nobody of importance'*."

I may well have uncovered a whole new member of the SS, but the deliberate concealment of his identity would cause us a problem, how do you investigate a man whose very existence had been covered up over fifty years ago? The reality of what I'd found was both interesting and frustrating at the same time and I needed to let the Simon Wiesenthal Centre know what I'd unearthed. Working on the basis that two heads are better than one, I shared all I knew about Hugo Drexler. Returning back to Eichmann and the problems I'd encountered previously, the dead end was still presenting itself to me, how would I climb out of this hole? The only way I believed I could was to utilise the one thing that had offered any solid information in the first place, the Belsen Files. I decided to go through all the information I'd gathered on the case, hoping there was a possibility I'd missed something.

I re-read my notes from my meeting with Sarah Davies and recognised somebody of importance may have been at Belsen with Drexler, someone also being deliberately kept under wraps. She'd told me Drexler was always with another man in the camp, and mentioned four *others* had been shot attempting an escape: no mention of Drexler's companion. It was clear from what she said and what Captain Roberts had told us that Drexler had succeeded and, I guessed, so had his bosom buddy. But was I walking down another blind alley – all I had was an enigma?

I was seriously thinking of closing the file at that point and moving onto a more solid case, something Fin had done whilst investigating Irma Grese and it had been a change of direction which had opened up a line of investigation into Ilse Gerver, the spoils of which we were now exploiting.

The problem was, I just couldn't let go. I had to find out what I could about the other German at Belsen, who he was, what he was and why he was there? Was he the 12th man? Could it possibly have been Bormann?

I went back to Eichmann and the ratlines, going over and over the evidence presented at his trial but the question kept gnawing away at me – 'Who could this man have been?' One thing was clear, it wasn't Hitler. He was too well known and wouldn't have been able to hide himself at a Charlie Chaplin convention. Even Sister Sarah would have known who Hitler was but the likes of Bormann and Mengele were then unknown to anyone who hadn't had close contact with them. Eichmann had disguised himself well at the time and I wondered who else could have camouflaged themselves at the downfall of Berlin.

Word came through from Kleinman, Fin's tame FBI agent and hacker. He'd been able to access more files Kaspar Stahnke had elaborately encrypted. Apparently, Stahnke wasn't as clever as he thought he was. Even though our ex-informant, before his demise, had insisted his computer would only open if his fingers were on the keypad, he hadn't taken into consideration this guy would copy his file prints onto 'gummy fingers' – artificial digits, easily made of cheap and readily available gelatine.

It would be me that would spend the next week, almost twenty hours a day, reading through file after file, trying to extract some kind of evidence from within that might identify Drexler or provide useful leads. If I found a relevant document written in German, I'd obtain a translation from a local translator. It was long winded but luckily Kleinman eventually found a file with a folder in it he thought I should take a look at.

The documents opened and I flicked through page after page with speed. "What are we looking for exactly?" Fin asked casually, looking over my shoulder.

"Anything on Drexler. I'm trying to see if I can find something related to his name, or Eichmann's. You making a coffee? Bring me a latte, no sugar, will you?" I replied and turned back to my monitor.

Fin left me alone as I trawled through the file. Eventually, I called him back into the room.

"Have you ever heard of the Secret Doctrine of the Thule Society?" I asked, Fin shook his head. "Nope,"

"Well, it's all in here: history, doctrine, the lot. It was a form of freemasonry and although, in itself, the 'Lodge' didn't have Nazi tendencies and a lot of their people were put into concentration camps, certain German members used the clandestine abilities to further their own causes and came up with the Thule Society. Its ideology was Popularist, Anti-Communist and Anti-Semitist. Here, look at this. It's the emblem they used, similar to the Swastika."

"What's the relevance of all this?" Fin asked.

"Well, early on in its existence a list of members was circulated. It's in this folder. It's like a 'who's who' of early NSDAP members and influencers: Rudolf Hess, Alfred Rosenberg, Hans Frank, Julius Lehmann, Gottfried Feder, Dietrich Eckart, and Karl Harrer are the best known ones. We know now that these people went on to make careers in the Third Reich or at the very least were held in very high regard by Hitler himself. Eckart was acknowledged to have been Hitler's mentor. What I'm thinking is, what if the twelve disciples were Thule members, later ones, from the period when they were more guarded and secretive? Stahnke had this file and information for a reason." I saw the lack of recognition in Fin's face. "And what if they were?" was all he said.

"Look, Fin, the Thule Society was an occultist group with a range of ideas, none of which, from my reading, were particularly healthy. Like many groups wishing to influence people they had a thing about the number twelve. Twelve signs of the zodiac, twelve months in the year, twelve apostles and in Greek mythology there are twelve superior and twelve inferior gods. Himmler was an ardent occultist and had places for 'twelve knights of the SS' at Wewelsburg Castle.' What's with twelve?

"All I'm suggesting is our 'twelve disciples' could have been members of the Thule Society, a society which is documented as having been a huge influence on the Nazis. Anton Drexler, the guy in the clipped photo we found with Bormann, moved in these very same circles and Hugo Drexler's name is on our list. Thule even owned the 'Münchener Beobachter' which later changed its name to the 'Völkischer Beobachter', the Nazi Party newspaper."

"There's something there, Gene," Fin replied, laconically.

"Well, there's more. I went back over our research into those listed as 'Disciples'. Nine of them are documented as having held rank or honorary rank within the SS. The exceptions were Speer, who said he was offered it but declined and Kurt Blome who carried out biological warfare research on behalf of the SS. From 1943, he took his orders direct from Himmler.

"Now, we only have Speer's word for it that he turned the offer down, just as we only have his word for it that he planned to kill Hitler by introducing poison gas into the Bunker ventilation system. It's possible that both of them held undocumented honorary rank in the SS. I mentioned before, the 'Twelve Knights of the SS'. They had special places reserved for them at Wewelsburg Castle and then there's the 'Black Sun' mosaic there as well. A twelve legged SS rune. The more I think of it the more I'm becoming convinced the 'Disciples' and the 'Knights' are one and the same. If so, then that puts Hugo Drexler, and whoever his buddy at Belsen was, right at the heart of everything."

Later, I sat reading an article I'd found online, 'The second coming, the return that will raise the dead from the grave'. It was New Testament stuff, but I couldn't get Fin's idea out of my head. The Lazarus Project? It had to mean something, Stahnke had thought so and it all fitted into Hitler's disordered beliefs.

I started formulating ideas, what ifs and possibilities; it was fanciful and had no real basis within fact, but for the first time in my life I could see where conspiracy theories came from.

I walked into Greenwich towards McDuff's with Emil and took a cell call from Fin, he was now at home working on something he'd found, describing it as the Alpha and Omega.

"You gotta read this stuff, Gene. They actually believed they could bring back people from the dead. It's in one of the files you gave me. I was looking for something mentioning the Lazarus Project, digging for information and this came up. It proves they'd planned it, even though they lost the war the crazy bastards still had the plan in place," he told me, then he asked about Emil.

I told him what we were doing. "McDuff's?" came the response. "Yeah," I replied.

"That's good, Gene. He likes spending time with you, I think the old man thinks of you as a son," he commented. After the call, Emil and I enjoyed a few beers but I hadn't realised how stressed I'd gotten myself. I guess it can disguise itself well and creep up on you when you least expect it and I'd certainly felt that over the last few weeks or so, that was for sure.

Chapter 4

The Alpha and Omega

"Eugene get yourself down here, I've found a manuscript they call a 'Codex' inside the Alpha Omega file, the Nazi's were into this kind of thing, concealing information within old scriptures."

As I entered Idar Court, Fin paced the floor, he seemed agitated waiting for me. Before I could get into the study, he led me by my arm, excited by what he was about to tell me, taking me to his computer screen.

"Okay, here, a wartime British intelligence officer authored a report around 1942, it's within the file that holds the Codex. It says Hitler had a phobia and became increasingly paranoid within his speech making. The academic that wrote it believed Hitler had a 'Messiah Complex', which is a state of mind where you believe that you're a saviour."

I interrupted. "I'm pretty certain I knew that already, Fin."

"Yeah, sorry, well, this would feed into what we've uncovered about The Lazarus Project and the blood taking. It fits into the idea that Hitler believed in resurrection and that he ordered blood samples to be taken from high ranking SS officers including himself. He *believed* he was the Alpha and Omega." He paused, waiting for a reaction. I just said, "Go on."

"Right, well, there's been many claiming to be 'messiahs' throughout history but what *is* a messiah? Among the dictionary definitions I found is – 'a leader regarded as the saviour of a particular country, group, or cause'. But the word actually comes from the Hebrew word 'mashiach', the literal translation of which is 'anointed' and that's where religious concept comes from – the person 'anointed' by God.

"Now, Hitler was a cunning man, he projected himself as a saviour and was generally accepted by the German people as such. But he knew that religion played a huge part in German life and, although one of the aims of Nazism was to be rid of religion, they knew it was far too early in the game to upset that particular apple cart. So, he nurtured their beliefs, created the Reich National Church and did his best to coerce the clergy into compliance. You still with me?"

I nodded.

He continued. "Another definition of messiah is – 'one who is anticipated as, regarded as, or *professes to be a saviour or liberator'*. And that's exactly what he did, Gene. But, here's the thing. I think he got caught up in his own lying rhetoric and came to believe it. I think he wanted to write himself into the history books as the Christ of his time. The only problem was that, by 1944, time was running out so, I honestly believe, he started to seriously consider resurrection, for himself or his chosen successor." He opened an image on the screen, it was a cross of the Zodiac.

"This zodiac, it's the same as the one in Stahnke's files. At the centre, the sun, and around it are the twelve constellations it passes through within the year, it also shows the twelve months, four seasons, solstices and equinoxes. Ancient civilisations worshipped the sun, believing it to be God's only Son. On the winter solstice, which is on December 22, the sun drops in the sky and pauses there for three days when it's considered 'dead', then it starts its rise upwards by a single degree." He pointed at the screen in front of us.

"Because of that, and the fact that it lies above the Southern Cross which is just below the horizon but could be seen from parts of Africa and the Middle East, the ancients always said 'the sun died on the cross and was reborn after three days. Sound familiar? The sun, apparently, 'returned to life' in the early morning of December 25, when it began its journey north again and the hours of sunlight start to lengthen. Therefore, the ancients said that the SUN was born on December 25 and celebrate by decorating stuff with holly and mistletoe and feasting. That's what the internet tells me, anyhow. Explains one or two things though, doesn't it?" He gave me a wry smile before continuing. "Hitler and his cronies knew all this because they promoted and celebrated the winter solstice as an alternative to Christmas; just close enough to the day for it not to cause too much concern.

"The Nazis believed they stood alone in the fight against what they considered evil or darkness – the Jews and non-Aryans. They set themselves up as the goodness or light, and here's where it gets interesting. The widely accepted religions all believe in a fight of good against evil. Even Mithraism and Zoroastrianism have Ahura Mazda and Angra Mainyu, eternal opponents, the light and the dark.

"Nazism was to be the new religion and Hitler would be the new Christ, Gene. And here's where I think the symbolism fits in with what you told me yesterday." He clicked on a star chart. "Look, Orion's Belt, known as 'The Three Kings'. In Christianity they're known as 'the Three Wise Men' – a symbol of the birth of Jesus. If you follow the belt's line downwards you come to Sirius, long thought to have been the star that guided the 'Magi'. The 'Magi' were priests in Zoroastrianism and the word basically means 'wise men'. Who are the three wise men or 'kings' of the Nazis, Gene? That'd be Hitler, Goering and Himmler.

"Is it a mere coincidence that the sun wheel features heavily in Germanic SS runes? The Black Sun at Wewelsburg?" He began slapping the fingers on his left hand with the forefinger of his right as he counted off. "Twelve knights of the SS, twelve signs of the zodiac, twelve Disciples of Christ, four seasons, the Heer, Kriegsmarine, Luftwaffe and the SS, the symbol of the summer solstice is the sun *and* also the Nordic 'S' rune, known as the 'sowilo' rune, which the Nazi's renamed the 'Siegrune' *and,* as you know, the double siegrune was the symbol of the SS. Need I go on?"

I sat back fascinated by what Fin was telling me, not wanting to throw water on his fire because I couldn't quite connect our investigation to what he was telling me and although interesting, at that moment, I couldn't quite follow his train of thought and wondered how this helped me find Drexler.

"You don't get it yet do you?" he asked.

"No, I'm sorry Fin, it's fascinating but I've not connected the dots yet."

"Look, you've already made a connection between the Thule Society and the Disciples on Stahnke's list, *and* I think you're right about Wewelsburg. Those places for the twelve knights weren't for high ranking SS Generals. Let's face it, nearing the end of the war, they'd be struggling to find twelve SS Generals who were as committed as the people on the list. They were for the Disciples. I think they were entrusted with ensuring the money got to where it could be properly used and making sure the results of the DNA research were safely delivered so they could start the creation of a 4th Reich in preparation for Hitler's second coming," he pronounced.

Although it still sounded like a bit of a whacky conspiracy theory to me, it was actually making some kind of sense. Then I remembered something. "Hang on, Fin. What about this Codex? Is all this in that?"

He gave me a sheepish grin. "I think so. I expect it to pan out."

"You think so! How's that?"

"Well, it's an ancient manuscript, or at least purports to be and it's written in old German script, so with that and my Kraut not being too good, it's difficult to say with certainty but I took it over to our translator and they gave me a very brief overview from which I came to the conclusions I gave you. It's obviously a faked document, done by the Nazis but trying to give the impression that it was 'all foretold in ancient times'. It'll have been produced by the SS Ahnenerbe department."

It was making more sense now. "Ah, the old 'forefathers heritage' people, the ones who were faking all the ancient sites and making up history. So, what you're telling me is you think this would have been 'discovered' at some time, had the war been successful for them, and dragged out to substantiate Hitler's claim to messianic heights and, when the DNA cloning research had proved fruitful, to ready everyone for the second coming. I suppose in the meantime, they'd just tell everyone to keep calm and carry on."

Fin laughed. "Hey, that's a Brits saying, not Kraut."

I smiled back. "I know, I have it on a tea towel we bought over there. I just like it."

We left it there and went out for lunch. When we got back, Emil handed a slip of paper to Fin and told him Kleinman said he should look at his copies of Stahnke's files again. The reference was on the paper. The result was interesting.

Dr Rudolph Keesler had worked alongside Josef Mengele, and had killed cripples and dwarves then boiled their corpses in calcium chloride to break their bodies down so he could send the skeletons to the

Dahlem Institute in Berlin. The Institute was involved in pseudoscientific race research.

The fact he'd worked closely with Mengele was noteworthy, but he'd covered his tracks well, leaving nothing in his wake, no laboratory notes or manuscripts relating to his work were ever found. On trial at Nuremberg, he was convicted on witness testimony alone and was sentenced, with others, to death by hanging. The sentences were carried out on 2nd June 1948.

The file Fin had trawled through identified a son, Marlon Keesler, but seemingly nothing else. We ran it through file recovery software Kleinman had recommended previously and found a fragmented document from which we were able to read a partial address.

Emil was keen we follow this up. Frankly, I wasn't sure it could be worthwhile but he was insistent. "If Fin's contact has given us this it probably leads somewhere. It may be a dead end but we have no option. So far, these files haven't shown us Stahnke had much time for rumour and speculation. Perhaps, all roads lead to

Rome but you'll never know unless you follow them, Eugene," he'd said with a smile.

Fin looked at me, I could see he was thinking what I was – if we could get someone else to carry out this going nowhere 'investigation' we could go back to our research.

"We'll need a little assistance with this one, Emil," he queried.

"We'll be fine, Mr Quinn. Leave what you're doing now and make your enquiries. I have every confidence in you boys but if it gets too much I can always come out of retirement and help you," he offered.

"What retirement?" we said in unison.

It didn't take too long to convert the partial address into a meaningful one and, after discussing the matter, we tossed a coin. I lost and had to be the lead man on a trip to Louisiana, the last known address of Keesler junior.

Our options weren't many. We could go for the pleasant approach, seeking his assistance and maybe get lucky and he'd tell us something useful or, if he looked like a ballbreaker, we'd have to bluff, but we'd need something to back it up. Several phone calls later and a trip into the Big Apple to see some ex-colleagues from NYPD and we had some old copies of Federal warrants to play with.

On a cold, wet day in November, we set off to JFK Airport. At New Orleans International, we picked up a couple of lease vehicles for the remainder of the journey to Jackson Point, the place where Marlon Keesler resided on a bend of the Mississippi 24 that crossed the Buffalo River. I'd go in alone, with Fin staying well back in the van with the blacked out windows.

As I approached the rundown homestead, two pick-up trucks sat on the driveway, one of which was being off loaded by a young man who noticed my approach. He didn't look much more than twenty.

I opened with – "Is this the Keesler residence?"

"Who's asking?" he replied.

"My name's Eugene Kennedy, I'm working on behalf of the FBI," I told him. I thought it may put him off guard a little. "I need to speak to a Marlon Keesler and I need to do that now, son." I wanted to keep his thinking options down so kept it firm and slightly forceful.

"I'll go get him," he said, wandering back toward the house.

Marlon Keesler wore black rimmed glasses, a baseball cap and faded denim jeans. The hat looked like it disguised a receding hairline. He had a strong jaw line and piercing dark eyes, the sort I'd seen before in others of his kind. I'd pretty much made my mind up about him at that early stage, there was an intensity I didn't like about him, an underlying confidence – he reminded me of the actor, Gene Hackman.

"What do you want?" he asked without ceremony.

"I just need some information from you, and we haven't the time for fooling around so I'll get straight to the point." It was bluff time. "Your father left you a file of documents a while back and I need to see them."

"Have you got a warrant with you? Because if you haven't, you can turn right back around and get the hell off my land."

That one sentence told me a lot. "Yeah, I've got a warrant alright, but I thought I'd give you the opportunity to work with me a little, you see the seriousness of the situation could leave you in all manner of trouble if you don't comply with my requests," I showed him my fake paperwork and let him read it. Hell, no one really knows what the genuine article looks like anyway.

When he'd finished, I said, "Now, seeing as I've got your attention Mr Keesler, can we stop jerking around? You know exactly what I'm referring to. I don't have the time and I certainly don't have the patience for any bullshit." I made sure he knew I wasn't about to be messed with.

"I haven't seen them in years, why don't you come on back tomorrow and give me a little time to take a look around the place," he tried palming me off.

"We've tried to keep this low key for your benefit but I'll tell you what I'm going to do right here and now," I said, looking back at where Fin was parked in the distance, Keesler following my gaze. "I'm going give you five minutes to locate those documents then, if you're still jerking me off, we're going to tear your house apart, piece by piece if we have to, until we find exactly what we're looking for. This is no joking matter, Mr Keesler, your compliance is something I neither need nor care for." I pushed my jacket back as I placed my hands casually on my hips, exposing my holstered sidearm. "Do we understand each other, sir," I said.

I smiled at him. "Ok, I'll get them! *You sons of bitches*! Coming here like this, in front of my boy, on my own driveway. I want your name and your badge number," he spat out.

"I've told you my name, it's Eugene Kennedy and I don't give a rats ass what you think, I'm here to do a job, to obtain the paperwork and I'll get it one way or the other, do you understand that, Mr Keesler." He hadn't finished bleating at me. "I'm not responsible for my father's actions, especially not fifty years ago, I've tried to sweep all that under the carpet and build a new life for my family here, then you turn up like this waving a gun around on my driveway, like some hot shot. How the hell did you know about these documents in the first place? Nobody's ever asked about them before, and as far as I know nobody knows they even exist."

"Well, I haven't waved the gun around, not yet anyway, Mr Keesler, but I take your point. However, that's information I'm not at liberty to disclose, hell, I could go to jail if I did. I'm sure you wouldn't want that. I *can* tell you that these documents may have vital evidence needed in bringing people to justice and wilful non-disclosure of them would be a Federal offence. I'm not absolutely certain of the penalty but I'm pretty sure it's probably five to ten years."

He turned to the boy. "Rudi, get up in the loft and get that old briefcase out of the trunk and bring it here, son."

I didn't want Marlon mulling things over and getting brave and asking more questions, so to keep his mind occupied, I engaged in casual conversation; the pick-ups, the homestead, what a fine boy he had.

When Rudi returned, I told Marlon, "Is this everything? Because if it isn't we're only going to have to come back."

"Yeah, that's all of it. I looked at it once years ago. Didn't like what I found but couldn't get rid of it somehow. It's not much of a connection but it's the only one I've got with my father." I was starting to feel sorry for him when he looked up and over my shoulder so I turned and saw we'd attracted the attention of some of his neighbours.

"Now get off my land, you son of a bitch and don't ever come back here again!" he balled. "You've got what you came for. Next time, I'll be ready and waiting!"

As we drove back towards the airport, I thought I'd handled the situation pretty well. My skills at bluffing were still intact and I'd secretly enjoyed the moment he crumbled into compliance, it would have meant my walking away with my tail between my legs had he not. Obviously, putting on an act and blustering had gotten him somewhere with his neighbours but underneath it all he was a fearful man. I'd probably done him a favor, taken a weight off his mind. It was the same for many children of Nazi war criminals, they didn't like what their fathers had done but they couldn't face the ultimate betrayal of volunteering their guilt or their whereabouts, preferring to keep the dark secrets within as a last recognition of a 'love' they'd once held.

I'd gotten the documents and that's all that mattered. We had a brief look through them but it wasn't the right time or place for a concerted effort so after dropping the hire cars back, we boarded the return flight to JFK and began to flip through them with more focus.

There were names. Keesler had documented his work with twenty doctors in Auschwitz, people like: Eduard Wirths, the chief SS doctor in overall charge of the medical experimentations that Mengele had performed, Horst Schumann of Block 30, which was the women's hospital at Auschwitz, who would forcibly sterilise victims who then died in awful agony because of the radiation burns they'd received. Block 10 was mentioned, a place where they experimented on woman's ovaries. Maximilian Samuel and Wladislaw Dering, two prisoners who were doctors, had been noted as present in one particular procedure, as was Keesler himself. I scanned through the documents, trying not to overlook anything of importance, but the adrenalin in both of us was dissipating rapidly. I found notes on Carl Clauberg, Johann Paul Kremer, August Hirt and Emil Kaschub and read of experiments conducted on prisoners. It was chilling, I hadn't realised the number of doctors that were involved in the systematic torture and annihilation of so many 'healthy' human beings.

I fell asleep on the flight, something I don't do normally, waking suddenly to the thud of a trolley clattering into the side of my seat. "I'm sorry, sir. Would you like a drink?" a female flight attendant offered.

I declined but it had pulled me from a dream. I tried recalling it, something about the 12th man and Drexler at Belsen. Could Keesler have actually been the 12th man or was it the man Sarah Davies had said was always alongside him? It got me thinking.

Back at Idar Court, we updated Emil with our findings and shared the documents. We left him with them, tomorrow would be soon enough for us, we both knew we needed some downtime. I went home to Jody.

The next day, we started bright and early, going back over what we'd already skimmed through *and* on to newer things. Keesler had been quite keen to document all he could. Had this stuff been available at his trial it would have saved the witnesses the torment of reliving the horrors.

Fin looked across the room to me "Hey, Gene, I've got something. Keesler was working on early experiments that identified traits of the genome specific to the race of a person," he said, waving a piece of paper at me. "This proves his work at Auschwitz was related to the eugenics programme and that alone indicates he was involved with their DNA research programme."

And so it went on. There were plenty of interesting leads to many names, some previously unknown to us, but nothing more in relation to our current lines of enquiry until I happened upon Keesler detailing a visit by a high ranking SS officer in respect of his and Mengele's eugenics research. It was obvious from the deferential tone used that this person wasn't just nosing around for fun. They quite clearly held the position of an 'overseer', a controlling force, possessing a respected knowledge of the research and, according to Keesler, they were pleased with the work being done, remarking that the material the Auschwitz unit supplied had permitted others to significantly progress the overall project's aims. As I turned the page, two names leapt out at me – *Das Lazarus Projekt* and *Oberführer Drexler*.

It didn't help us find Drexler or the 'twelfth man', but it confirmed, without doubt, two things. The Nazi eugenics research and the Lazarus regeneration project were inextricably connected and, seeing as the SS rank of Oberführer, or senior Colonel, was essentially an administrative senior post, Drexler held a position controlling that activity. *But,* we still had to find him.

Meanwhile, Fin had an appointment to visit and speak with Hans Baur's third wife, Crescentia, who'd agreed to discuss her husband's life story, having been convinced by Fin he was an author researching a book about Hitler's personal pilot. He'd even fed her the title of the fictitious tome – 'Hitler's Aviator'.

"Catchy isn't it," he'd commented before he left for Herrsching, Germany. In all, he spent two days in conversation with Baur's surviving wife and found nothing of any significance, however she did confirm that Baur had devised a plan to get Hitler out of the Battle of Berlin. He had a Fi 156 Fiesler Storch on standby which could take off from an improvised airstrip located by the Brandenburg gate. She also claimed Baur was the last man to see Hitler and Eva Braun alive. The interviews had taken place at her home and Fin remarked, on his return, that her living room had been almost filled with photographs of her husband in his military uniforms, some of which pictured him alongside Hitler. Others showed him with Himmler, Ernst Röhm, Speer, Bormann and Rudolph Hess.

Fin commented, "She was a pleasant old girl but her nonchalance was quite spooky at first, given what we were surrounded by."

That's how it goes in this game, not every line of enquiry is profitable.

Chapter 5

The Research Bureau

Tilmann Modell had come to Emil's attention, an SS accountant at Auschwitz and later Belsen; our boss had been doing a little private investigation of his own and accidentally found his name written somewhere. It woke a spark in him then ignited a fire. It seemed he had some prior knowledge of Modell who was SS and in overall charge of the money and valuables taken from the occupants of the incoming trains at Birkenau.

"I want to know if this man is still alive, he will have handled money stolen from the people of our ghetto and it's common knowledge that these men pilfered items of jewellery to utilise after the war. This takes priority over everything, Eugene! He stole from the inmates, he was there when I was!" he said, with a tremor in his voice. It was clear he was trying hard to keep himself together and that this was obviously a subject close to his heart.

I stood looking at him, not knowing what to say. I knew Fin wouldn't be pleased at yet another case being thrown into our hands, distracting us from what we believed were our primary enquiries, but I knew we couldn't put this one down. I was going to do it for Emil. If I worked closely with him it would leave Fin free to carry on with our current research. Should we discover Modell was still alive, I knew Emil would want to be in on the arrest and I'd need to be nearby to protect him from himself. My first port of call would be the documents from the Belsen Trials – in there we'd find if he was prosecuted or not.

I sat in the study with Emil close by, believing we'd be working through the night but it didn't turn out that way though. We found evidence of Modell's death pretty quickly and it pre-dated the Belsen Trials. He'd died following a serious illness whilst incarcerated in prison, in Hameln, the town made famous for its rat catcher, *der Rattenfänger.* We suspected it was before he could be indicted, simply because we could find no record of prosecution evidence against him. He'd escaped being served justice, unlike the other 156 war criminals who were hung, the women singly, the men in pairs. Hameln had a new Pied Piper – the hangman, Albert

Pierrepoint. It was a bitter sweet discovery. Although pleased that Modell was dead, I could see Emil was frustrated that he hadn't got to look into the eyes of the man who'd played such an important role within Auschwitz-Birkenau whilst Emil himself had been there. He stood behind me looking at the words on the computer screen and a tear trickled down his cheek.

Fin walked in, breaking my train of thought. "The Shroud of Turin, the thing they reckon Jesus of Nazareth was wrapped in after his death? Well, it was tested and they found a blood group on it, AB positive and it's referred to as 'Golden Blood'. Oddly enough, Drexler's blood group we now know is AB positive."

I interrupted. "Lots of people have that blood group, Fin."

He smiled. "You're right, Gene, but 'lots of people' aren't the subject of our investigation. At the moment it's just an observation but I don't believe in coincidences where these people are concerned. I've been looking into it and the Nazis had ties within the Vatican who could have given them access to the shroud."

"Where's this leading to?"

"It's just an idea. What if the Nazis had tested the shroud and knew the blood type on it? I wouldn't put it past them to then claim that Hitler had an AB positive blood type. It fits with the resurrection narrative."

I was intrigued. "Do we know Hitler's actual blood type?"

He shook his head. "I'm pretty certain his personal physician, Morrel, would have known, but you try finding that information anywhere. I can't and I doubt you will either, it's just not there. For some reason, it seems to have been airbrushed from history." He shrugged his shoulders. "It's just something to think about. I'm off for a coffee." I joined him.

In the kitchen, we mused over the amount and diversity of inquiries we had gotten ourselves into and Fin suggested we were 'the Research Bureau'.

"We're not from the FBI but we are from *the Bureau*," he said, laughingly. By the time we were ready to go back to work, that's who we'd decided we were – the Research Bureau.

I'd been working on leads to Mengele, he'd become a naturalized citizen of Paraguay and resided in a village called *Hohenau* near the Argentine border. With that in mind, thinking that Drexler may have followed the same routes he did, I trawled through the internet and found that at the turn of the century some early settlers in that area were listed as '*Dresslers*', it caught my eye, could there be a link between the families, did Drexler have family ties in Paraguay? Did Mengele settle there with the knowledge that Drexler would be following? I needed to get feet on the ground in Hohenau.

Before I could put that into effect, Fin updated me with information he'd found in a book titled '*Eyes of Auschwitz*' by Hans Hesse.

Karin Magnussen was a biologist, and was employed by the Kaiser Wilhelm Institute on the 'Eugenics Programme'. Her particular interest was eye pigmentation (Projekt Augenfarbe) which fell in line with the Institute's post war population policy based on the racial ideology of the Nordic race. In essence, her experiments were about changing the color of people's eyes. She initially used a Sinti family of gypsies, from the village of Mechau, North-East Germany, who had a high prevalence of one iris being a different color to the other or one iris being two different colors. At first, she would administer drops of adrenalin to their eyeballs but later she had the entire family deported to Auschwitz-Birkenau. As she was only a civilian, she had no access to the camp but she knew someone who did – Josef Mengele. He would carry out further experiments for her, injecting not just adrenalin but also other substances including atropine then, when he thought the time was right, he killed them and had the eyes sent to Magnussen so she could dissect and study them. She was never put on trial for war crimes, although her work on the eugenics programme put her in direct contact with Mengele. She was, however, fined 490 Reichsmarks for 'opportunistic membership' of the Nazi party. She was an avid Nazi supporter who wholeheartedly embraced the national socialist movement but somehow, after the war, was classified only as a simple 'fellow traveller' as opposed to a Nazi. You could only surmise this was because some agency within the Western Allies were interested in her research

He concluded. "Gene, she'd have probably known something about Drexler, given what we think his status within the research system was, and at the moment, she's living in a nursing home in Bremen, Germany."

"And nobody's ever tried to interview her?" I asked.

"I don't think so Eugene, but *we* could try."

It didn't take us too long to find the place and Fin took on the responsibility of arranging a possible interview. I was pretty slick at bluff but Fin was better with bullshit.

"There's something I've been meaning to ask you, Emil."

"What, Eugene?"

"I thought I'd read or seen the name Tauber before somewhere. I got to thinking about the Belsen trials and how it said that guards commonly worked in both camps; with that in mind I did a quick check. It appears there was a Tauber in Auschwitz, SS as well, do you recall such a name?"

"There were a lot of guards at Auschwitz, Eugene, you paid attention to the ones closest to your block, many names and many guards," he said, contemplating his thoughts. "But I suppose I may have, it's a long time ago, and the name Tauber is quite common, there must have been at least one of them there."

"But you're not a hundred per cent sure?" I pushed.

"No, I can't honestly say I am. You remembered the actions of the guards more than their names, you'd recall a beating or a face, even if they were ten blocks away, you'd learn to keep clear of such people."

"Okay, I'll dig a little deeper, maybe I can find something about him that may trigger a memory," I said.

I'd sent flowers some weeks earlier to Sister Sarah Davis in respect of her lost friend Deena and followed that with a letter updating her about the case as I'd promised. I'd mentioned names, including Juan and Héctor Tauber along with several others. I'd thought nothing of it at the time other than saying thank you to an old lady who'd given me a push in the right direction which had helped us move forward a little.

Then I received a call from Emil. "I've just spoken to a nurse in England named Laura, she works at 'Rose Cottage' where your witness Sarah Davis lives. They're quite close, apparently, and she told me how Sarah received a letter from you updating her on the case. She says Sarah wants to talk to you about something real important, she's recognised a name within your letter, a name she knew, and needs to tell you about it. The name was 'Tauber', 'Héctor Tauber'. The line went quiet for a few moments, I thought Emil had wandered off as he often did.

"Are you taking this in, Eugene," he asked.

"How the hell does she know Héctor Tauber, Emil? Never mind, I've got a feeling about this, I need to go back to Stodmarsh and while I'm there I can have her take a look at our uncropped photo of Drexler."

"Your enthusiasm for your work is commendable but I haven't quite finished yet, I have more, Eugene. It seems Sarah recalls treating our unknown German, who had a badly infected lesion on his face that had gone septic, a large laceration above his right eye likely brought about from the butt end of a rifle. She's had her nieces look through some paperwork from her war records they kept for her when she went into the home and they've unearthed a list, made at the time, of people she treated on various days. There's only one that matches the exact description of injury and treatment and that name was Tauber," he told me.

"So, Héctor Tauber could well be our unknown German and I didn't suspect a thing."

"It doesn't matter, Eugene, the important thing is we've got something to work on now, don't dwell on mistakes you haven't made. He must have felt very comfortable and been a really good actor to slip past your keen eye. The only thing is I can't figure out why his son Juan would have approached you in such a way *if he knew* about his father."

"Maybe Héctor's lies were so good that his own family don't know about his past," I responded.

First, I needed to go back to Stodmarsh and get a positive identification of Héctor Tauber, luckily his son had taken a souvenir photograph of our meeting. I'd be able to utilise that and hope that fifty years hadn't changed him so much that Sister Sarah couldn't identify him.

Then, I had to revisit San Fernando to see what information I could get Héctor Tauber to tell me but I realised if I blew my cover he'd close up on me and any chance of discovering if he was the 12th man or finding Hugo Drexler could be lost forever. It wasn't going to be easy and I needed to plan it very carefully. Then I remembered Héctor had mentioned Drexler was known as 'the forgotten man'. Who'd first coined that nickname? Surely, they must have had some knowledge of the man or of his circumstances. Also, he'd said he knew 'of' him but what if he'd lied and knew him much better, the nickname originating from that knowledge. I'd missed that at the time but it all knitted together now. If the two Tauber's were one and the same, there was the answer.

Emil was excited by the news, he knew I was onto something big but warned me to be cautious. "You have to treat Héctor Tauber as the frail old man he's portrayed himself as and at no point must he suspect you have information on him that betrays his true identity. Work on an approach and reason to go back, if he realises you've come back without one, he'll know your intent is him," he offered and I understood.

Then he hit me with – "I'd like to come with you on that trip to England, Eugene. I think it's time for me to start pulling my weight around here," he said.

I tried to put him off. "You're retired Emil, or supposed to be, it's a long flight and it would be uncomfortable for you."

"Yes I know, but I've been to England before, Eugene, and it's a nice country. I think I'd like to take Luiza with me. You spoke highly of the Red Lion public house and the accommodation, so, well… I think we'll tag along, see how things pan out," he flashed me a smile, the one that was hard to resist.

"Okay, it's your show, but I can do this on my own if you want a holiday with Luiza," I offered.

"That's appreciated and I'll keep it in mind, you're a good boy, Filip, you do a fine job. I was only commending you to Luiza the other night before we went up to bed. I think she already knew though," he informed me with a grin. Once again, he'd just slipped his brother's name into the conversation as naturally as could be, he'd not even noticed. I just accepted it. I knew he felt comfort in my company and at his stage in life with all he'd been through I just didn't have the heart to correct him, besides in some way I think it gave him a little contentment. Apparently, I looked like his brother, so Fin had told me, maybe he just got a little confused now and again.

Good to his word Emil joined me on the trip to Stodmarsh, accompanied by Luiza, who'd be great company for Jody whilst Emil and I visited 'the old girl'. The flight was again long and tiresome. I gave Emil some of the crossword puzzles Jody had brought to bide the time away.

The hire car was a pleasant drive and we arrived at the Red Lion Inn late that night after a traffic jam on the M25, which I'd later learnt was a common occurrence. It put the lid on one hell of a day for us all. When Robert the landlord greeted us we were all but done in for the night. He insisted we had a night cap. Again his hospitality stood before him and to be honest I was ready for some of those English beers after a long day of travelling.

We sat around the fireplace as he let us know about the comings and goings of the village that day. A local Morris Dance troupe had descended on the pub, it was their annual pilgrimage to Stodmarsh and they were called 'The Black Morris' and were quite frightening by all accounts; faces daubed in black and foreheads swathed with yellow and white handkerchiefs whilst they performed their 'dance' which from Robert's description was more of a musical attack with sticks. Later, they'd come inside the pub to drink and talk with the locals, more than willing to inform anyone who enquired about the tradition.

I watched Emil sit quietly listening to what was being said, noting his concentration. Afterwards, he informed me he'd witnessed something similar with Luiza when they'd paid a visit to Krakow a few years earlier.

Sleep came easy that night, the beer had done its work and I fell into a deep slumber quickly.

I always seemed to be in the confines of Auschwitz since I'd met Emil Janowitz and this was no different.

The little bird watched from the barbed wire as the Kapo Pleva kept prodding me in the chest with his baton, provoking a reaction, harder and harder he rammed the stick at me until it felt like I was being punched. I wanted to hit back but knew the consequences, the SS guards were watching close by and I had a brother to think about, so I just took it. It was humiliating being treated that way but I'd gotten used to my surroundings and what came with them. I stumbled to the floor, which was a mistake, it left me unguarded and vulnerable for just enough time for the heel of Jarmil Pleva's boot to catch me in the eye, I felt the blood immediately. I rolled myself into a ball for protection from what was about to come. I first felt a kick into my stomach which emptied the wind from me, then a punch to the head which buried me deep in the mud and the hand that followed, sunk me deep into the mire. Unable to breathe I fought for air, my chest pounding and my lungs feeling like they would burst. I thought I would die in the mud but instead of flailing around to get out of the strong grip that held me under, I did nothing. I had no strength. I accepted my fate.

Pleva stood above me, "Get up, and get to work little pig," he called then released me. As I raised my head, the little bird stood on the ground before me, chirping, then flew away. Gasping frantically for air, I woke with a start to repeated knocking at the door. "Breakfast in twenty minutes you two," Robert announced.

The sweat had poured from me in the night and Jody asked if I was feeling alright. Too often now, my dream world was a very strange one. How did I know this name, Pleva? A small sparrow that skipped, cheeping, across the windowsill made me recall the little bird that had watched me with curiosity then, when the Kapo gave me final respite, had turned and flown away. I needed a shower.

We met for breakfast around eight am, after which Emil and I set off down the lane towards Rose Cottage to meet Sister Sarah. We were greeted at the front door by a young lady I'd not seen before, after letting her know our intent, she invited us in to the foyer of the building to wait whilst she went off to find Laura, the nursing manageress. We were shown through to a conservatory where Sister Sarah sat looking out into the garden, watching birds feed from a pole. I noticed blue tits and gold finches. I'd become somewhat of a bird watcher and had gotten used to their types, I guess the little friend of my dreams was the reason behind that, curiosity had gotten the better of me and I needed to know what type he was; finding that out became important to me.

"Hello Sarah," I said, passing her a bunch of flowers Emil and I had bought in the village earlier. "It's nice seeing you again, thank you for the call and for the information about Héctor Tauber, it's of great importance to our investigation. This is Emil, my boss, he's the man I told you about."

"Oh hello, Emil, thank you so much for the flowers they're beautiful," she responded.

Emil gave her his best smile and said, "Here are some chocolates as well. Jody, Eugene's better half, chose them for you. She says they have lovely soft centres." She accepted them, setting them down on the small table by her side. "Eugene's told me about you, Emil. It must have been an awful experience in Auschwitz, but you look so well now for a man who's been to the gates of hell and back."

"Thank you, Sarah, Eugene's told me about you also, he says you still have a glint in your eyes and I can see that. He tells me you're a mighty fine lady."

Just then Laura came in with a pot of tea, three cups, milk and sugar on a tray and a plate of Sarah's favourite biscuits alongside.

"Shall I be mother? I learned that one from Monty," I told her. "I've been meaning to use it for some time now." Emil looked at me, enquiringly. "I'll explain later," I mumbled out of the side of my mouth.

"Sarah, we've brought a photograph taken not too long ago when Eugene went to Paraguay on a little adventure a few weeks back. He met a man called Héctor Tauber and we're just curious that you seem to have treated a man called Tauber at Belsen all those years ago. Take a close look at it; do you wear eye glasses? I think you'll need them. We were just wondering if it could possibly be the same man."

He passed her the photograph, which she looked at through her glasses with pensive eyes. The frown on her face had me a little uneasy, she wasn't identifying him as easily as I'd thought she might.

"Is this the only photograph you have of him, he's a lot older, it *is* fifty years ago and my memory isn't what it used to be. I can recall him as a younger man but seeing him fifty years later is a lot different," she said, turning to Laura. "Do you have my magnifier, dear? You know the one I use to do the crossword with?" she asked.

"It's in your room, I'll go and get it," Laura replied. She left and we continued our conversation.

"Have you been out lately, Sarah? Still taking the herbal medication?" I winked.

"Ooh yes. I love the Mad Cat ale, it's a lovely little treat for me now and again," she replied in a knowing manner. "We'll take you down for some lunch later if that's alright with you, the ladies are just out on a walk around the village, it'd be nice for us to all meet up," I said.

"That would be lovely, I don't get out as much as I'd like to nowadays, old age is a terrible thing you know, Eugene."

Emil interrupted, "Tell me about it Sarah! I find myself in rooms I don't recall a reason for entering all the time nowadays. I just stand there wondering to myself, '*What the hell am I doing in here?*' Luiza looks after me though, you'll like her, she's my wife, has been for more years than I care to count. She often mentions how it doesn't feel so long," he said with a mischievous look on his face. "I always tell her it seems a lot longer, sweetheart," he laughed.

"You're terrible, Emil," she chuckled, just as Laura returned with the magnifying glass. Holding it toward the picture, she observed, "You see that faint scar here above his right eye, that's what I was looking for, the laceration I tended to all those years back. I knew if it was him, the scar would still be present and the pockmarks you see on his face were caused by shrapnel. I don't recall how he came about them but I dug a few pieces of metal out of his cheeks. He was a lucky boy, it could have taken his eye out," she commented.

"So, you're sure this is the Tauber you saw at Belsen, Sarah?" I asked.

"Yes, as sure as I can be after all these years," she replied.

I needed a bit more clarity. "But is this also the same man you saw always in the company of Hugo Drexler?"

"Oh, yes. Did I not say that before? Yes, he's the man I would see in company with Hugo Drexler."

"One more question, Sarah, before we take you to lunch." I took out the uncropped photo of Drexler and his brother with Bormann. "Who is this man here?"

"Why, that's Hugo Drexler! A few years younger than when I met him but wasn't he handsome?" she replied, a twinkle in her eye.

"That's fantastic, just fantastic, Sarah. Time for lunch, I guess," Emil responded with a big grin.

Our trip to England had been a success, Sarah was quite a remarkable lady, age had caught up with her but you could still see the athletic young woman she'd once been. As before, I promised to keep her up to date with the investigation. I told her she was a big part of the team now, which satisfied her greatly. I wanted her to feel a part of what we were doing, she deserved that.

Chapter 6

Karin Magnussen

Fin set up a meeting with a former work colleague of Karin Magnussen's, Rena Keller, who for the last seven years had been collating information about Magnussen's work. He'd arranged for our visit to take place at the former Nazi scientist's nursing home where she now resided in Bremen, Germany. He'd applied for an interview with her, which had been granted, and Keller would interpret between Magnussen and ourselves on the understanding that we were compiling a paper for the 'New Scientist' magazine. Resourceful as ever, Fin used his connections with several journalists to authenticate our story.

After the war, she'd spent over twenty years as a Biology teacher in Bremen, living out a normal existence. Now in the twilight of her years, at the age of 88, we were permitted an audience with one of Josef Mengele's close but little known collaborators.

I spoke with Emil prior to the meeting, knowing the loathing he carried for people such as Magnussen. "I know Eugene, I promise to be professional, the greater good must come out of this, I know it's not about me, and I do understand your concerns."

Not commonly known to the outside world, Magnussen had identified deported children and families to Josef Mengele for him to experiment on in line with her own research and in doing so had just 'happened to mention' that if they died then would he kindly send her their eyes for dissection. Whilst others had believed she wasn't aware of what was happening at Auschwitz, it was clear to us that she did. We'd even found a reference in the Belsen Files that simply said, 'Magnussen at the Institute knows' and we already knew about the collaboration between the Kaiser Wilhelm Institute and Auschwitz Concentration Camp.

We arrived in Bremen, after a difficult journey. There'd been several delays but my somewhat jaded spirit was energised slightly by the hire car brought to us in the car park – a silver C-Class Mercedes. I sat in the driver's seat contemplating the assignment ahead and its significance to the case we were investigating.

I turned to Emil. "We need to extract what we can from her, there's no advantage to be gained in breaking cover and laying fault, we already know Magnussen's crimes. Our line should be one of curiosity and an inclination to listen to her explanation of the work she collaborated on with Mengele. The fact she granted us an interview says she's willing to talk." He was in agreement and quite relaxed about the whole thing.

Approaching the entrance of the nursing home, I saw the word 'Sanctuary' was cut into the stonework above the front door. I thought about it and its meaning, people in danger of persecution usually sought sanctuary. That significance was wasted here.

We were led into a room where a frail faced old woman sat in a chair drinking black coffee. To the left of her sat a slightly younger woman, possibly in her late sixties wearing spectacles, greying hair. I noticed a pile of notes on a table in front of her that she appeared to be randomly organising. As we entered the room, she looked up then stood, holding a hand out to greet us.

Rena Keller, a dreary looking woman, introduced us to Karin Magnussen who remained seated with a look of curiosity on her face. I wondered if she knew who we were and what we were there to do.

Unexpectedly, Magnussen spoke in faltering English, "You are here to ask questions about my work, I believe?"

"Yes, Dr Magnussen, we want to understand how your work began, the hierarchical system the scientists used and what the work actually involved, the projects, etcetera, if you don't mind?" I replied.

"Please, sit down," Keller offered. "Dr Magnussen speaks very little English, I think it best I translate any questions you may have for her."

On the outside, Magnussen didn't appear to be the monster we'd taken her for and her voice betrayed a different character altogether. Most of the individuals we'd come across in our investigations hadn't looked or sounded like butter would melt in their mouths; evil has a way of disguising itself.

Keller held notes in her hand but spoke freely. "Dr Magnussen and the other scientists didn't work in an instructed fashion as Mr Quinn suggested in his letter. Scientists don't work like that, they work in collaboration with one another; more work gets done that way. In the same respect, Dr Mengele wasn't an overseer of Dr Magnussen's work, they worked alongside one another, within their research," Keller explained. Magnussen nodded in agreement.

Emil responded with a quiet confidence. "That's interesting, you may be able to help me with a few questions we're working on regarding the eugenics programme, particularly how you identified racial origin?" Keller translated then replied, "It was of great interest at the time. In her research, Dr Magnussen found that specific proteins could help identify the origin of a person but work was being focussed mainly on the war effort. Many scientists were tasked to create a virus that could attack the immune system but Dr Magnussen was allowed the freedom to pursue her own interests and research." The woman alongside her nodded agreement, clearly understanding what was being said, and added, "Today, there is AIDS, this was such a virus. Many believe this was also manmade."

I decided to throw something different into the conversation. "You didn't work alone though did you, there were many other scientists and as you quite interestingly say there didn't seem to be much of a hierarchical system. It must have been difficult not having a system of order in place but would I be right in assuming Drexler and Keesler ran the Lazarus Project, or would that have been a venture you were all equally involved in?"

Magnussen looked at me with curiosity. I smiled innocently back, confidently awaiting her answer. Keller broke the ice that was developing between us. "I believe they all worked together on that particular project, as with all of the other assignments. I think I'm correct in saying this, I have it in my notes somewhere," she said, somewhat flustered, then turned towards Magnussen for guidance and received a reassuring nod. This simple act not only confirmed our suspicions about Hugo Drexler but also that Magnussen's English was better than she was admitting.

Emil and I had decided earlier we wouldn't mention anything about 'eyes'. We didn't want Magnussen getting overly defensive and hoped that by doing so she would lower her guard. She'd acknowledged the Lazarus Project but our plan was not to linger there, we wanted to chip away at it bit by bit, we thought an all out assault on the subject would lead to a termination of the interview.

"You worked with blood it says here?" Emil enquired.

"Yes," she replied.

Magnussen touched Keller on the knee to get her attention, they spoke quietly then Keller translated.

"Dr Magnussen says, it's fascinating what you can establish from a tiny droplet of blood. Dr Mengele used to send samples for her to analyse, to identify any abnormalities or deformities in a specimen, and the reasons for them. She says it was a very strange period of time, people look back and have opinions of the work she was involved in and see it in a certain way, but at the time it was cutting edge science and quite normal to practice in such a manner. In essence, they were endeavouring to work collectively to eradicate specific genetic flaws within certain races, they had an abundance of material to work with," Keller said.

Quietly, under his breath, Emil muttered, "*Yeah, human beings.*" I stood on his foot deliberately to quieten him. Keller was quick to reply. "Yes, they used the deceased. These experiments would never have taken place beforehand but it was a time of war and many people had died. They believed it would be advantageous to utilise the bodies for the advancement of medical science."

I knew she was being economical with the truth but I accepted what she'd said. We were getting what we'd come for and I didn't want to stop the flow.

The two women whispered together then Keller turned and said, "Dr Magnussen says, she was aware that some were working on the idea of a biological weapon. It was an idea before its time but she left the project long before its completion and, anyway, it was interrupted by the ending of the war but she does know they were trying to make a perfect virus, one that could be manipulated at will."

"Did they test it?" I queried.

"She believes that, at some point, it was tested in the camps, mainly Dachau. The prisoners were injected and their reactions observed and noted."

"Did people die?" I realised it was a question I shouldn't have asked as soon as the words came out of my mouth.

Keller looked at me sternly. "Yes, Mr Kennedy, I believe many," she replied angrily. "But, Dr Magnussen played no part in that. The Führer ordered that the science had to continue," she insisted. "The Frau Doctor moved on to other things."

I thought it time. "Dr Magnussen, it was normal procedure for high ranking officials within the SS to have their bloods taken, did you work on those blood samples and could you confirm that DNA was extracted at the same time," I asked and waited patiently for the reply which eventually came after much whispering.

"She says, no to your first question, she mainly worked within the field of specific ethnic groups, but that's not to say other scientists did the same. She says you're correct in your assumption that DNA was extracted, there was a lot of new science being done at the time, science which, may I remind you, has benefitted mankind greatly," Keller replied.

I looked toward Emil fearful he was about to say something untoward but he didn't, he was controlling himself as promised.

"I have a question about a man we know as Héctor Tauber. Do you recall that name?"

Magnussen shook her head.

It was time to make a few things up and hope that some, at least, hit the target. "Well, we *know* he worked on the Lazarus Project, some people have suggested he was a cytologist or a physicist or even a chemist. Does that ring any bells for Dr Magnussen?"

Keller translated. I noticed Magnussen mulling something over in her head; she began whispering in the ear of Keller once more.

"Not with that name. There was a chemist who worked closely with Dr Drexler and Dr Mengele during the Frau Doctor's short stay with the project."

"Can she recall a name?"

Magnussen had understood the question. "His name was Johan." Anticipating my question, she smiled, "It was my father's name. Let me think a while." We sat in a silence which turned to awkward silence. I was just about to end the torment when she said, "Wernicke. Johan Wernicke. Yes, I'm sure, but I was told years ago he had died."

It seemed Tauber was a dead end so I continued with: "My colleague, the one who sent you the letter, is following a line of investigation into Martin Bormann, he's not convinced of his demise," I said.

Keller responded, "Mr Kennedy, Martin Bormann died in 1945. What can science possibly gain from an investigation into him?"

"It's not so much Bormann," I persisted. "It's more the idea that comes out of the question, the idea being the Lazarus Project." We were back on subject.

"What has this to do with the work Dr Magnussen performed, Mr Kennedy?" Keller looked at me inquisitively.

"Well, we've a lot of stuff we need to piece together to understand the science behind the projects that Dr Magnussen was participating in and if she was involved in one of the greatest scientific experiments of the 20th century, it would be a crime to waste any of that information," I replied, doing my best to fake an honest face, hoping to play to their egos.

Another hurried discussion then Keller replied, "You must remember, Mr Kennedy, Dr Magnussen was in a position of war when all of this took place, things always look worse in hindsight. Lazarus was a concept they were endeavouring to bring to life, the idea was to create a pure race and the science of Eugenics was the new religion of its time, it had countless possibilities but the war took priority and today within modern science some of those ideas have saved countless lives."

"So, it was about creating a 'Master Race'?

Magnussen cut in. "I prefer to say 'a pure race', Mr Kennedy."

"Tell me about the twelve Disciples?" Emil asked abruptly.

"The twel... the twelve..." Keller stuttered. "I'm not sure I understand what you mean," she finally replied, looking curiously at Magnussen.

"The Twelve Disciples," Emil encouraged.

The two women whispered together then Keller replied, "She says it means nothing to her, it's something you must know more about than she does."

Emil had jumped the gun but I could tell from Magnussen's eyes that she was lying so probed a bit more. "Dr Magnussen, we have information regarding twelve people who were referred to in a document as the 'Disciples'. They either escaped via the rat lines to South America or were hanged in the trials that followed the war," I told her.

She looked confused but it didn't strike me as lack of knowledge. It looked more like fear. She'd probably believed that after fifty years all of this would have gone away.

"I'm wondering if those gentlemen took her work with them, one of the greatest experiments in the last hundred years. Wouldn't you have thought they'd have wanted to protect that work?" I asked, looking at Keller.

"I'm sure they did, Mr Kennedy, but I doubt Dr Magnussen knows anything about that," she replied.

"Could you make sure she understood the question?" I asked.

"I understood it, Mr Kennedy," Magnussen replied, turning to Keller to speak amongst themselves in hushed tones.

"May I see your credentials again, Mr Kennedy," Keller asked.

"Yes, by all means." I took the card Fin had given me earlier that week from my wallet, the telephone number and address of the New Scientist's head office were neatly printed on it, along with my details embossed across the top. Magnussen examined the card, turning it over analysing what she was looking at.

Not wanting to give either of them too much time to think, I continued, "I apologise if my questioning is a little thorough but I want to get things correct for our article, your work was quite unique, at the leading edge, not just of its time. We just want get a true understanding, especially of what must, surely, be considered the definitive science research programme of the 20th century?"

Another private discussion; Magnussen nodded.

"Is there anything else, gentlemen?" Keller said.

Emil replied, "If you don't mind, yes, I've a few more questions. We're aware that samples of blood were taken in the bunker before the downfall of Berlin, we strongly believe from Hitler himself. Did you ever work on the taking of mitochondrial DNA from bone fragments and were the samples you worked on blood group AB positive? That was Hitler's blood group, wasn't it? And finally, one last question I must ask, did you work on the cloning programme with the other scientists?"

I'd been hoping to ease these subjects into the conversation before Emil had shoved his foot through the 'door' but it was too late now. We got the result I expected.

"Gentlemen, Dr Magnussen is getting very tired now, she'll try to answer your final questions but we really must call it a day. She is, after all, eighty-eight years of age and this cooperation has been very exhausting for her."

I stood up and tapped Emil's arm to do the same. "That's fine, we appreciate the time you've given us, and I hope Dr Magnussen is fully rested soon," I responded, knowing Emil wouldn't extend that gratitude.

The two women talked in the doorway as a nurse waited to take Magnussen to her room. Keller returned to Emil and his questions. "Your question about mitochondrial DNA? She says no she didn't. Adolf Hitler's blood group was 'A positive' and she says she only knows this from a conversation with Dr Morrell, his physician. Your question about cloning? Yes, it was a field of research they were working on at the time, but the premature ending of the war cut short the project. Now, if that's all gentlemen, I'd like to make sure Dr Magnussen is settled in her room." Her immediate departure ended all thought of further interaction.

As we left the 'Sanctuary Rest Home', we passed through a yellow rose garden; the flowers were in bloom. Emil paused and stared up into the foliage of an old oak tree that sat in the middle.

"What's the matter, Emil?" I asked.

"Look, Eugene, it's him, he's here." His hand pointed up towards a branch of the tree. The sun shone through the leaves making it difficult to focus but after a few moments my eyes readjusted and saw a bird looking directly at us, the sunlight bouncing off his beautifully coloured wings. His gaze never left us, we were the center of attention; I got a feeling he knew us and we knew him in return. He looked like the little bird who sometimes visited me in my dreams. Suddenly, there was a strange feeling to the air, a change in pressure or something, I felt it but Emil seemed unaffected. "Not yet, little one, we have work to be done," I heard Emil whisper. The bird chirruped heartily and flew off.

It hadn't gone as well as I'd wanted but we'd answered the question about Drexler's association with Mengele, a simple nod of the head had disclosed he worked alongside both Mengele and Keesler, also herself, but Keesler was the only one that had been served justice.

Fin's investigation into Bormann was still on my mind, the question remained – would it tie into our investigation in some way? I made a call to check on any progress.

"Gene, I've got something for you. I've found a correspondence sent from Mengele to the Kaiser

Wilhelm Institute, it seems to be a routine progress report of some sort. It's headed 'The Lazarus Project' and its distribution list has the following names on it: Eichmann, Barbie, Rauff, Stangl, Blome, Brandt, Bohn, Bormann, Drexler, Schumann, Grawitz and Speer, all names on Stahnke's 'Disciples' list. It confirms that what we've uncovered so far is authentic.

"I still don't know who the twelfth member is, but I've eliminated Adolf Hitler as a possibility for two reasons. Firstly, I discovered from a report made by the CIA in 1945 that Hitler's blood type was A."

I interrupted: "We've just discovered that ourselves from Dr Magnussen."

Unfazed, he continued, "Secondly, and most importantly, Hitler believed himself the Alpha and Omega, that's to say the Messiah of his time, therefore we can conclude he would hardly have considered himself a disciple, and that leaves our twelfth disciple ambiguous. It begs the question why are Schumann and Grawitz on the list and in the loop. Maybe they were first reserves? I don't know, but I'm surmising there must have been someone of great importance to Hitler that he wanted as the twelfth disciple, and that's if he even knew about the list in the first place. "Anyway, with that I started looking at religion and everything I could find about the original disciples, who they were and so forth. It took me a long time but then I found, *'Jesus then sent her to tell the other apostles the good news of his resurrection.'*

"It's talking about Mary Magdalene and it's in the Gospel of John, Eugene. *'The other apostles'* clearly indicates that she was considered as one of them. The word comes from the Greek word apostolos – 'person sent' and Jesus, according to the Gospels sent her to give the others the good news."

"Great work finding the memo, Fin. So, you think the twelfth disciple could be a woman?"

"I don't know, Gene. It's got to be considered but I was trying to make sense of it and started to try to walk in Hitler's shoes for a while, trying to think how he may have thought. Who would be his Mary Magdalene? If this is all about resurrection and *if* Hitler was in on it who, if anyone, would *he* want brought back? And if it was simply just about bringing *him* back, who would he entrust overall responsibility to because it would have to be someone who was passionate about *him personally*, not just his politics."

"Did you come up with any names?"

"Plenty, maybe too many. There's his mother of course, Klara, who he spoke of in saintly terms and *maybe* Eva Braun, but there were others too like Ilse Pröhl, Hess's wife, who was fanatical about Hitler. Helene Bechstein loved the younger Adolf like a son, she bought him a Mercedes costing 26,000 Reichsmarks and called him her 'Wölfchen' – little wolf. Then there was Winifred Wagner, the daughter of Richard Wagner who Hitler greatly admired, there were rumours of marriage but I found something that said they fell out over the persecution of the Jews. In the end it was the questionable nature of Hitler's relationship with Geli Raubal and her mysterious death that drew my attention. This was a woman Hitler obsessed over, he loved her and, putting things into context, it's plausible that Geli Raubal could have been the Mary Magdalene figure within Hitler's twelve disciples but I still have my doubts."

I interrupted again, laughing: "Is that because she shot herself in his Munich apartment in 1931 in order to get away from his possessive grasp, Fin?"

"Laugh all you want, Gene. I was coming from Hitler's point of view. Apparently, he never got over it and never understood why she did it. Anyway, more food for thought and probably way too much, I admit. How did you get on over there?"

"We got some confirmations about the Project. Drexler and Mengele were working closely together, same with Keesler but she didn't recall Tauber. Not a glimmer of recognition of the name and I forgot to bring the photograph. We did get something I hadn't expected. It seems Hugo Drexler had a string to his bow we didn't know about. He was a fully qualified scientist in his own right. She referred to him as Doctor Drexler. Obviously, his overseeing 'Lazarus' wasn't just based on his connections. Also, she told us the Nazis were researching and testing a bioweapon, some kind of virus that they could mutate at will. She claimed it got interrupted by the end of the war but maybe that explains why she was so casually treated by the post war justice system."

"Imagine the consequences if they'd achieved that goal," Fin replied.

"I wouldn't want to, oh and before I forget. See what you can find on a Johan Wernicke. It's just a name she mentioned."

Shortly after our visit, in the February of 1997, the woman who collaborated so closely with Josef Mengele and directed many of his genetics studies, died in her nursing home in Bremen.

Born into a middle class family, she became a fervent National Socialist, lecturing on racism and demographics but she never apologised for her work or gave up her beliefs and was known for stating the Nuremberg laws hadn't gone far enough.

Maybe she knew she was dying and needed to feel some kind of atonement for what she'd done, otherwise I couldn't figure out why she let the interview run so long as she had. Sure, granting it could have been simple ego but I kinda felt, during the time we spent together, that she had guessed what we were up to. She told us stuff she didn't need to, she could have just claimed a very bad memory. I hope that was what she was doing, for her sake. Yep, we'd been lucky with our interview, a couple of months later and we'd have missed our opportunity.

"The Registrar at Mengele's wedding in Uruguay," Fin said, when we got back. "What do you think about us arranging a meeting with her and seeing if she can identify the photographs of Tauber or Drexler as being amongst those present at Mengele's wedding?"

"Not a bad idea. Emil's got the money and it might just come up with a good result," I replied.

"How about you and I go out to see her?" he asked.

I knew he hated being office bound now that Emil had decided to do a little more field work so I readily agreed.

"How are we going to keep him occupied, though? He's starting to get a real taste for travel?"

Fin smiled. "I trawled through the Belsen Files and found a guy right down Emil's street. Yasiel Liebermann, deported from the Warsaw Ghetto when Emil was there. An accountant in his previous life he made it to Kapo at Auschwitz. Emil might even have known him or, at least, of him. He worked with Tilmann Modell so it says, and you know how he got fixated on him."

We sat organising interviews in priority order, Ilse Bernatzky should come first; we could do it en route as it were. It made sense. If she identified Tauber, it would give us something to use in our conversations with him. We also had to dig a little deeper on the names Fritz Ullman and Helmut Gregor; the false identities Mengele had used. What if, once he'd ditched them, someone else used them for a while? All it would need was a change of photograph and they had a temporary new identity which bought them time. We'd look at 'Ricardo Bauer' as well – reputed to be Bormann's alias, what if it wasn't his but Drexler's? We had to explore every avenue, if you didn't you'd never know if you'd missed something.

We took Emil out to McDuff's and gave him our news. He enjoyed his three beers. He never bent that rule but always told Luiza he'd had two. "You have to take a little pleasure from life sometimes, Eugene. What my wife doesn't know won't hurt her," he'd remarked on the way home. I suspected Luiza knew exactly how many he'd had.

I stayed over in Idar Court that night. Jody was on a night shift anyway, so Emil and I sat up until the small hours talking. He was good company and we spoke about the significance of the little bird. He told me he'd realised it appeared each time someone within Auschwitz came into his life, then he sat wondering about that for some time before saying, "Maybe, he's there to take them to the garden of good and evil." Most people would think his words crazy, but for some reason I didn't.

Chapter 7

A Haunt of Jackals

The planned visit to Ilse Bernatzky was shelved; Fin had spoken to her on the telephone and discovered her grandson worked for Netscape in the States. She supplied his details and we made contact. No problem, he'd said, we could send him what we had and seeing as he was returning to Uruguay shortly as a surprise for his grandmother's birthday he'd sort everything out for us. We sent him the uncropped photo of the Drexlers with Bormann and the recent picture of me with Tauber. We waited, anxiously, in anticipation.

When he got back to us, we were hit with a bolt from the blue. Yes, she could identify Tauber as having been at Mengele's wedding although she hadn't known his name. She couldn't recognize Drexler, his photograph had been taken some 15 years before the marriage. Included in the email were some pictures taken at the ceremony. It turned out it was an indulgence of his grandmother's to obtain a picture of everyone she'd married, if possible. Most people had no problem with this and would post a copy out to her but if they declined she would have her photographer friend, who touted for work at the venue, take an 'illicit' one. It was two-fold thing she'd said – it ensured she had a pictorial record of her work and, she'd told him, "If they refused, it made me feel they had something to hide and I wasn't going to get myself in trouble with the authorities."

We opened the attachments to find three black and white images of the wedding party, taken surreptitiously. Tauber featured in two of them with others, one of which contained Mengele and his bride with Tauber alongside but slightly further back. He was smiling and appeared to be in conversation with another man, his hand on the other's arm. We couldn't be 100% certain but the likeness was there. Who else could it be? We were pretty sure we'd captured the image of Hugo Drexler.

It was time I paid Tauber another visit. I'd arrange it through his son, Juan the pharmacist, and telephoned the number we'd exchanged. Our plan was to feed Héctor Tauber with just enough information so he believed our focus was purely on Mengele's last known location, which in turn would aid us finding Drexler, something he was already aware of. But, as Fin once told me, the only plan that ever works is 'the plan will change as and when necessary'.

The former chemist of San Fernando was adept at throwing the scent from his trail and we believe he'd used his son for years without him ever knowing it. I'd figured in a place like San Fernando, a chemist would be the eyes and ears of the local area so he had to know something more than he'd told me originally, now I knew it.

We met Juan at the bar on Garibaldi Street. I'd brought an American baseball shirt along as a gift, he'd previously mentioned he was a 'Red Sox' fan and as a child had followed the team with great keenness on the black and white portable TV set they had in the drug store back in the 60's. He'd told me his all-time hero was Rico Petrocelli who wore the number six shirt. I picked the same numbered shirt up in a New York sports center for twenty five dollars. As I gave it to him, I could see the delight of the young boy he'd once been.

"Wow! Thank you, I've always wanted one of these," he'd said.

After introducing Fin, I told him we wanted to know some things about Mengele and Eichmann and needed to ask his father a few sensitive questions and felt Héctor may not want to answer in front of him.

"I'm not sure he'd want to burden you with such things, so if it's alright, and with your permission, we'd like to see him alone at first," I'd said, knowing the baseball shirt would have already made me the day's most popular person as far as Juan was concerned.

On the morning we met Héctor Tauber, it was a bright, sunny day. We sat in the same living room I'd been in just a few months earlier, the photograph of Juan's mother, Eliana, still on the fireplace mantel, undisturbed. I smiled as Tauber re-entered the room with a tray of iced water.

I cast off with: "First of all, thank you for allowing us to come and visit you here today, Héctor. We're hoping that some small piece of information tucked away in the back of your mind may help us find something *you* may think unimportant but which may just piece together something of significance to us and help us find the last known sighting of Dr Mengele.

"Any tiny snippet of information you may not think important may just connect the pieces we already have. We've interviewed a registrar, a lady by the name of Bernatzky, and her records are the last known confirmed sighting that we have of Mengele and *others*. It was at his wedding, in Uruguay, fifty-eight, I believe." I watched him for a reaction, there was none.

"It seems there were quite a few guests, you know, friends, maybe relatives, and we're trying to ascertain if Hugo Drexler was there as well. This would have been in a town called Nueva Helvecia. Does any of what I've just mentioned bring back memories?"

"I'm sorry, Mr Kennedy, I only knew Eichmann in passing, and I didn't know who he was until the Israelis kidnapped him and as for Drexler, I've told you already, I knew of him but never met him. Dr Mengele, I never knew and as far as I know, he escaped, did he not? Mossad didn't want to risk losing Eichmann at the time by continuing to chase Mengele and I only know this from what I've read. But, I've told you all of this before. I understand you may think I have something more but really, I have not. There is nothing more I can offer. I'm an old man now and when you get to my age you tend to forget a lot of things."

I'd been hoping he might feed us something useful just to get us out of his hair but he'd decided to cling to the master plan – I know nothing.

Something told me that if I continued on my current course he'd stick to his script, so, the plan changed. I took the Mengele wedding photo from my jacket pocket and added an embellishment.

"This is you, Héctor. It was taken at Mengele's wedding in 1958. We have two witnesses who confirm it was you. Take a good long look. Even we can tell it's *you*."

He took the picture and as he did I saw there was a slight trembling in his hand.

Fin interjected: "Let's stop jerking around, Héctor, or should I call you Johan?"

Momentarily, it was like someone had slapped his face. Only for a second but it had been there.

"Yep, that's right, Dr Wernicke. We know exactly who you are, so let's not waste time." Fin leaned forward menacingly and spoke quickly. "I will make your Reich a heap of ruins, a haunt of jackals and I *will* lay waste its towns so no one can live there. Do you know my role in life, Dr Wernicke? It's to find people like you who've evaded justice for too long and serve them with their just rewards."

Tauber had started to go pale, so pale I began to worry that he might keel over and die on us.

Before I could say anything, Fin continued: You're not even Jewish! Your wife was but not you! You married her as a cover, to make yourself appear Jewish. I mean, who'd look for a man with a wife so very clearly Jewish *and* with a name like Tauber?" Fin was up and pacing around.

"There's just one thing that's bothering me though, your son Juan? He doesn't have a clue does he? You've used him as an errand boy all these years. Did you see Eugene watching Eichmann's house and send your boy to do your dirty work for you, Herr Doctor?"

"My name is Héctor Tauber, my birth certificate is in the draw over there," he said pointing at a bureau, but it lacked any real conviction.

"Yes, we know all about birth certificates. You can get them anywhere if you need to. You married Eliana to disguise your identity and you know who Hugo Drexler is because you escaped from Belsen Concentration camp with him, didn't you?" Fin glared at him.

"I married my wife because I loved her. Don't you *dare* sully her memory and keep my son out of this. He's a good boy, he doesn't need to know any of this; he works hard. He's all I have left in the world." Fin had definitely hit a nerve.

I briefly placed my hand on his knee, as an act of comfort, and said, "I have no doubt your son is a good man, Héctor. He's a loving, caring son with a good heart who'll be devastated when he finds out about all this. It's pointless to try to go on with the deception. We have another witness who has identified you, a nurse who treated your wounds in Belsen, do you remember her? That's when you adopted this alias, isn't it, at Belsen. Tell me how that happened?"

And suddenly, he simply surrendered. He almost looked relieved. Haltingly, he said, "We were on an inspection visit. In the panic to get out, we got left behind. We knew if we were caught, as high ranking officers, we would be blamed for the mess that was that awful place. We broke into the stores and changed into uniforms we found there. When the British asked for our papers we just said we'd lost them."

"Where did you get the name Tauber from?"

"It was a name I must have heard somewhere. It was the first thing that came to mind when they asked me. I told them I was Johan Tauber."

"Were you not attacked by the inmates?"

"No, when the British came we were in the SS blocks outside the camp."

"Why didn't you flee the camp before they came?"

Fin cut in. "Because they didn't want to be mistaken for Waffen SS fighting troops and engaged by trigger happy British forward units and the only other way to go was east. Not much of a choice, Eugene."

Tauber nodded.

I looked at the sad figure of Héctor Tauber. Or should I be thinking of him as Johan Wernicke? I had to ask. "So what happened when the British entered the camp?"

"They saw the state of the place, the condition of the inmates, the dead and dying lying all over and started beating us, rifle butts, fists, kicks and then a British officer arrived and simply said 'That's enough' and they stopped. Later, we were sent to the nurses for treatment and made to move the bodies of the dead and dying."

I was intrigued to know how they managed to escape. His reply, for some reason, chilled me. "You have heard of the 'Werwolf' organisation?" We nodded. "They infiltrated the camp when forced labor was used from the nearby villages. They had contacts..."

Fin interrupted, "Die Spinne?" Tauber nodded.

I still had the photograph in my hand so I showed it to him again. "There's someone else in that picture; the man you're smiling at. You have your hand on his arm, surely a gesture of intimacy. We both know who it is and you do as well, don't you, Héctor? It's Hugo Drexler, isn't it?" He nodded again. "Yes."

Juan entered the room. "What's going on, Eugene? I leave you alone for a short time whilst I chop some wood and the neighbour tells me she heard raised voices," he asked in a worried tone.

"Juan, I'm sorry but I think you need to ask your father if he has anything he wants you to know."

Héctor squirmed in his seat. "Please, he doesn't need to know this," he whispered to me.

"Know what?" Juan asked. The room was silent.

I looked at Héctor. "Either you tell him or we'll have to. He deserves to know the truth."

He beckoned Juan to sit down and, when he had, he said to him, "I was an SS officer, working for the scientific department in the field of biochemistry." Juan looked at his father with confusion on his face, I felt pity for him; in the short time I'd known him he'd shown himself to be a doting son and a good man.

The old man then told him, and us, everything he could before saying: "It was a long time ago, I changed my life, my past was something I had no choice in. I wanted to advance science and at first I didn't know what they were doing. I was told they were natural deaths. By the time I realised the truth, it was too late. I had committed myself and saw the end justifying the means. Drexler convinced me of that and he was a very persuasive man. So many sins but we had no choice, we knew we were so close to achieving almost a miracle. I'm sorry, Juan. I tried to keep this from you but I knew, in my heart, one day somebody would come walking through that door."

Juan interrupted, "My mother?"

"I loved your mother, very much. She showed me the truth about myself, she made me realise what we did, what I'd done, was wrong."

"She knew about this?"

"Yes, Juan. She knew. But, we put it behind us; she loved me just as much as I loved her."

"But all those people, innocent children, and you've hidden those crimes all this time."

"I promise you my son, I didn't kill anybody, I swear on my life."

Juan turned to me. "You were looking for him all along, weren't you?"

At that moment, I felt I'd betrayed him. "No," was all I could manage.

Juan suddenly became very composed. "Do you have enough evidence of what you're accusing him of? Are you going to denounce him?" he asked.

"We were never looking for your father, Juan. It just happened, but we came to believe he knew Hugo Drexler. That's who we're looking for. They escaped from British custody together and we think he knows what happened to him, after he disappeared from this area."

Turning back to his father, he said, "Papa, it was you wasn't it? The monster in the dreams you told me about as a child?" Héctor lowered his head in shame.

"What do you mean by that, Juan?" I asked.

"When I was a small boy, he would tell stories of bad men, soldiers in the war killing men, women and children. He made me believe they were somebody else, he warned me to stay away from Nazi's. He told me, they are all around us here and I wasn't to get involved with any of them, he told me they did very bad things."

I nodded understanding. "Look, my colleague and I need to just discuss something. I'm hoping it'll be of advantage to you both." We stepped out of the room.

"Jeez, Fin, why didn't you tell me you'd found out he was Wernicke?" I hissed.

"I didn't know he was. All I found from my checks was Wernicke qualified at Münster University and then went to work for the Institute. I've been waiting for a contact to get back to me. I reckon his SS rank was just honorary, anyway. One minute he existed and the next he didn't. I just thought it was worth the bluff or are you telling me you're not happy with the result?"

"Yeah, alright, it worked. Of course I'm happy. The thing is – what are we going to do with him now? I don't know about you but I *actually* believe him. The way he reacted to you accusing him of marrying his wife as a cover, the honesty in his voice when he told his son how much he'd loved her."

"Gene, have you been reading romance novels again?" He paused. "Ok, to be honest, I'm with you on that. What about we offer him 'cooperation and immunity'?"

"Fine, but in future, anything else that you *know you should tell me,* then try your best."

Back in the room, we made the offer. Héctor hesitated; I guess old loyalties were strong. Juan leaned over to him and said, "Do it, Papa, do it."

And so he did. At the end, he said, "I stayed behind here because I'd met Eliana, and I had settled. I could have gone, following the trail they left me but my name, as you suggested, was something I could use to disguise myself. Eliana knew I was SS. When I knew I was in love with her I had to tell her about my past but she never betrayed me to anyone. We lived in a village for many years, and we didn't see a lot of people in those days. My wife believed that under the uniform, a good man existed. I didn't kill anybody, Mr Kennedy, I swear. It's the reason I had the confidence to risk staying behind when the others left. Besides, Eliana said, quite firmly, she would not run and I, Mr Kennedy, Mr Quinn, would not leave her."

"Why here? Why Buenos Aires?"

"A big city, many places to hide. Mengele was living here and enthused about it through the contact organizations. In the early years, I'd gone to one or two gatherings where I met Mengele and also Eichmann, but never on the same occasion. They were meeting openly; no fears at that time because no one was really looking for them. Die Spinne was planting false stories in the press to deflect attention. These were old comrades meetings, or so I thought, but it became obvious in a short time that the politics and visions still very much existed. I didn't go to any more.

"Then, not long after we'd moved to this house because we had Juan on the way, I discover Hugo Drexler is living here. I went to the bar and there he was, sitting at a table on his own with a beer. We acknowledged each other, nothing obvious and no one noticed.

Despite the fact back in the old days I'd counted Hugo as a friend, I just didn't want to get involved with him again. I knew where it would lead, *'come with us, we can build a new Reich'* and as I told you he could be very persuasive. I avoided the place until I found out after they took Eichmann, fearful he'd be next, he'd abandoned the house and left the area. That's why the locals named him 'the forgotten man'. He left but no one came looking for him."

"Did he try to find you?" Fin asked.

"Not in person. But I was stopped on the street one time by a man who told me *'Hugo says Nueva Helvecia, July 25th make sure you are there, it's important'.*"

"So you're telling us, Drexler followed Mengele to Uruguay, specifically to Nueva Helvecia," I queried.

"Yes, for the wedding and after, I don't know what. I went as requested. Don't ask me why, I was curious. Once there, I found it was the marriage ceremony and I spoke with Hugo. We had a few drinks and he tried to drag me back in. Mengele even offered to employ me as a salesman for his family firm which was operating out there. They wanted me to act as a courier. I refused, telling them I couldn't leave my wife for long periods, making things up about a difficult birth and a sickly child. I told them things had changed with me. We parted on good terms, I felt.

"Look, all I know is a group stayed in Buenos Aires. I'd made a point of avoiding repeated contacts with these people but one of them was Drexler. He wasn't here long. Once Eichmann was taken, he was afraid he would be next."

Héctor Tauber could have been arrested by the Argentine Federal Police but we decided that for now we'd leave him be. Should we need to go back for more information or clarification, we'd have his and Juan's complete attention and support.

Sometimes principles had to go out the window, for the greater cause. We had a mission to complete.

Our last sighting of Mengele was in Nueva Helvecia, Uruguay, but his body was exhumed in Sao Paulo, Brazil, buried under the name of 'Wolfgang Gerhard'. Apparently, he'd drowned whilst having a stroke in a resort named Bertioga. The identity of the body was eventually irrefutably confirmed in 1992, from DNA testing, to be Mengele. The problem for us now was we didn't know where he'd been in between. If Drexler was, for some reason, following Mengele then our trail had gone cold for the time being.

We had to make a decision about the direction of our enquiries. Should we follow Fin's investigation into the Bormann sightings *and* connections or follow the Drexler inquiry. I was as passionate about my cause as Fin was about his. We talked into the small hours one night and it was Fin that offered a solution.

"What if I allowed you guys to concentrate your efforts on finding Drexler and I utilise my time trying to figure out the links between Mengele, Bormann, Hitler and the Lazarus Project," he suggested. My argument against that was, from everything we'd learned, Drexler virtually was the Lazarus Project. Héctor Tauber had told us, whilst explaining his involvement in it, that Drexler was often referred to as *'Herr Direktor'*.

In the end, Emil made the decision that Fin would conduct his own investigation into his subjects whilst he and I concentrated on Drexler *but* all Lazarus Project information had to be shared.

A few days later, we received a telephone call from Juan Tauber; his father had started telling him more things. "He's mentioned research they were working on and said it involved a cloning programme, implanting DNA into live subjects, using prisoners," he said.

"So are you saying they would replace somebody's DNA?" I asked.

"I'm a pharmacist, Eugene, not a scientist. You'd need to talk to somebody else about that," he replied.

Later that evening, I spoke with Jody; her job brought her into contact with people in the medical research department at the hospital. She told me, "You're talking about gene therapy or somatic gene editing which changes the DNA within the cells to treat disease. I doubt they were so advanced in those days. The changes made in the body cells would be permanent."

"So you're saying it's possible to change a person's DNA," I asked her

"In theory, yes," she replied.

"This re-opens a line of enquiry about Martin Bormann. If you can make a permanent change to someone's DNA maybe the skull recovered in Berlin is a DNA doppelgänger, manipulated or changed to suit purpose, which in this case would be convincing the authorities he was dead when he wasn't. Maybe, Fin has got something after all?"

"Maybe, maybe not. It's not nearly as straightforward as you might think," she answered casually, whilst chopping some carrots. "You have to find other family members who carry the same Y-DNA and or mitochondrial DNA. A first cousin would do."

"What's Y-DNA?"

"It's the DNA on the Y chromosome. It gets passed from father to son. If you're able to gather it then it would tell you, subject 'A' was the son or father of subject 'B', but it wouldn't tell you who he actually was, not all sons or fathers have the same surnames in day to day life."

This was starting to get complicated and Jody could see it all over my face.

"Look, Gene, the best identification is made from the nuclear DNA, the stuff that's passed from both parents. The problem is, if the remains have deteriorated so much that nuclear DNA can't be obtained then mitochondrial DNA is the go to solution but it only passes down from the mother. So, if you can test the subject's mother you can have a pretty good identification but it's no good testing a daughter because it'll only tell you who her mother is.

"Then there's the Y-DNA, which we just spoke about." She dropped the carrots into a pan. "*But* it's not always available in remains that have been subject to external influences like being stuck under earth and rubble for twenty years or more. So with only mtDNA you'd have to locate a relative who came from the same maternal line as the subject to make a pretty good identification. As I said before, probably a first cousin, a child of the subject's mother's sister for instance."

"How do you know all this stuff?"

"I sit at the same lunch table as the research guys and a couple of pathologists, Gene. Here, honey, hand me that pen."

She drew a sketch on a piece of paper to explain what she'd meant. It actually helped me get my head around it all, well nearly all.

I explained to Fin what Jody had told me and showed him the piece of paper. I wasn't sure if he took it onboard but he nodded in the right places and agreed with what I was suggesting. He listened patiently but I could tell he had something he wanted to tell me.

"Yasiel Liebermann, remember the Kapo I told you about?" he asked.

"The one from Auschwitz that turned up in the Belsen Files?" I replied with curiosity

"That's the guy, he's turned up in Merano, in northern Italy, the same village the SS used to escape. Seems to be popular with Nazis, Bormann's wife died there in '46," he told me.

"Yeah, seems so. There was former SS officer, Anton Malloth, condemned to death in Czechoslovakia for war crimes in Litomerice, the largest sub-camp of Flossenburg. He had a nice time in Merano and lived there quite happily for years."

"The very place, Gene, you have a good memory," he replied.

"What the hell is Liebermann doing *there*?" I enquired.

"His family run a bar near the town centre. He married a woman in the early seventies, opening a bar called *'Cristina'* named after his wife. Mengele's second wife, Martha, lives there too."

"I thought this was going to be an easy 'dead or alive' enquiry. The fact you've already found he's alive, in Italy, is starting to make things a bit more complicated. I thought the idea was to get Emil out of our hair for a little while so we could make progress and not have him blurting stuff out in an interview?"

Fin gave me a rueful smile. "Well, that's kinda what I thought but it seems I made the mistake of picking a name he knew."

"But didn't you tell me, sometime, Liebermann had already been dealt with for collaborating?"

"That's right, Gene, he served his time for his part in the war but Emil now wants him to have a personal visit."

"That means one of us is going to have to go with him!"

Emil walked into the room. "What seems to be the problem, gentlemen?" he asked.

"Nothing really, Emil, it's just the thing is, well, this Liebermann guy. Fin tells me you've found out he's served his time and we're hard pushed as it is. I've a number of interviews I need to get under my belt to push forward on the Drexler case and I just don't have the time *and* I don't have the inclination to even consider a visit to Italy," I said with more than a hint of exasperation.

Fin was about to speak but Emil interrupted him. "I see, Eugene. You think I want *you* to investigate this? Mr Quinn hasn't told you the full story then has he?" he said. "Sorry, Gene, you jumped in before I could tell you," Fin responded.

"It's a little job I want to do myself, Eugene, to reacquaint myself with a Kapo. It's how I originally got started in this line of work you know. I don't want you two taking your eye off the ball on the 'Lazarus' issue, this one is mine," he said.

"Well I'm sorry for jumping to conclusions, Emil. I'm just that wrapped up in all of this, it's taken over my life."

"I know, Eugene, it's been a hell of a year," he said with a grin then told us he planned to fly out to Italy the following week with Luiza whilst we continued our investigations. Colluding Kapos were Emil's thing, it was a big part of his life and I knew he'd never gotten over some of the things they'd done to survive.

The next day, Fin told me, "I've done a more thorough check of the Liebermann file. He did serve a sentence but what Emil omitted to tell us was somebody came forward after his release who'd recognised him on a TV news item. There was something Liebermann did at Auschwitz..."

I waded in. "What did he do that they'd missed?"

"Well, at the trial nobody came forward with the information they'd witnessed him placing Zyklon B capsules into the down pipes in the crematoria so he was only trialled for collaborating and some minor violations. He'd have hung if they'd known at the time, probably. Emil's got the details and the witness is still alive *and* there's a statement I missed in the records. He's kept it to himself, I reckon, thinking we'd interfere with his plans. When the evidence was presented around 1956, Liebermann fled before the police could arrest him, ending up in Merano, Italy. He was an Austrian Jew who happily collaborated," Fin said.

"So what do we do here? We've a ridiculous amount of work to plough through. Do we just let him do it?"

Fin shrugged. "I don't see what else to do, Gene. He's going to do this one way or the other and he's specifically tasked us to continue with our cases. I guess we just have to trust the old man with this. I'll make sure he updates us regularly. That's about all we can do, Luiza will make sure he doesn't push himself too far."

Even though I knew Emil was capable, his age was catching up on him, then again so was Liebermann's, he'd be well into his eighties now. In the end I had to go with Fin's way of thinking, we didn't have much of a choice in the matter, Drexler was my prize and Emil wasn't about to wait on this one, not for my selfish reasons.

Chapter 8

Rill of Death

Emil and Luiza flew out from JFK on the Friday after celebrating their wedding anniversary. Mission: 'to locate Yasiel Liebermann and bring him to the attention of the authorities for crimes committed within the confines of Auschwitz-Birkenau'. He'd spent the period before the journey delving deep into our own 'Sikora Files' and discovered Aleksy Markowski, his old mentor, had been thorough. Emil now had two statements and one live witness. All he had to do was find the other and the initial enquiries revealed they were last known at an address in Krakow, Poland. There was enough there, hopefully, to at least make Liebermann an undesirable alien in his hideaway, Italy.

I promised to look after their dog, Max. I'd done it before, taking him on walks across Greenwich common and on one particular morning I was reminded of the sign 'Arbeit Macht Frei' at the gates of the Nazi concentration camps; made by the prisoners on the metalworking labour details. A familiar welcoming greeted you on the gates at the entrance to the park. The words 'Greenwich Common' met you in the same crafted metalwork. Whilst Max scouted off around the park, I lost myself in my thoughts.

'Work Sets You Free'. How could they have possibly done all of those appalling things? If I didn't do the job I did, I'd believe it unthinkable, the masses that died in the Nazis bid to nurture and create a 'master race was a stain on humanity. The Holocaust, they called it – destruction and slaughter on a mass scale. Once, I'd looked the word up and found it had another, historical, meaning – a sacrificial offering that was burned completely on an altar.

The common was a peaceful place though, only your thoughts could disturb the tranquillity and the sign at the entrance frequently put me in that erroneous mindset, so much so I often entered the park from the opposite direction. The flowers were beautiful at this time of year and, in the spring, the smell of the lilac bushes would fill the air.

After our walks we would head back to Idar Court. This day we found Fin waiting.

"Emil called. His second witness is still alive, but only just by the sounds of it and Liebermann's gone, he must have caught wind of Emil's arrival somehow. I don't think he's in the best of moods, reckoned he'd had a wasted journey."

I thanked him for the news but something told me there was more.

"What else do you want to tell me, Fin?"

"I don't particularly want to tell you but Luiza called about ten minutes later, said he'd gone for a nap. It seems he found things out about Liebermann, things he didn't want me or you to know about yet. She did say he told her that Liebermann assisted Josef Mengele in the selection processes on the ramp at Auschwitz. Emil will have been through that procedure himself so I suppose to him Liebermann committed the ultimate crime, betraying his own kind. But she says, after fifty years of marriage she knows her own husband. She thinks it's something about his own family. Apparently, she'd pleaded with him not to go, but he insisted. Oh, and they're catching the next available flight back home."

I drove to JFK to pick them up. He looked pretty despondent. "I missed him by three days, just three days, damn it! God knows how he caught wind of me or where he's fled to now," he said, desperation on his face. It was more than disappointment, he was angry.

I'd noticed that creeping into him of late. He was normally quite a subdued man, the kind that wouldn't show his feelings to people he didn't know or trust, but lately he was acting differently. I wanted to know why and I had my suspicions of course, but didn't want to reveal them in case they were misguided.

"Who was he Emil, there's something you're not telling me?" I asked, nervously.

"Leave it, Eugene," he abruptly replied, again out of character for him.

"I don't mean to interfere, I'm your friend and if there's anything I can do to help, you know I'm here for you, you're a good man, Emil Janowitz," I told him. "*You have people around you that love you and don't like seeing you upset like this, a problem shared is a problem halved, so they say,*" I offered, a bit lame but it was all I had.

"I know, Eugene, sometimes the pain inside is just too much to bear and it feels like only yesterday when I stood on the ramp watching them walk away towards their deaths," he said quietly.

Suddenly, in that moment, I realised what he was talking about. "Oh Jesus, he was on that selection wasn't he?" "Yes, Eugene, he was," he said, lowering his head to momentarily hide the welling tears. "My mother and little Anna were no use to the Nazi's, try to imagine that, you're only use is fuel to feed the crematorium, the easiest option is to kill you. I found him within our files and put two and two together and found out he not only stood on the selection at the unloading ramps but was also complicit in dropping Zyklon B canisters through the hatch that stole the life from my mother and little sister. I don't have a choice, only I can get justice for my family, but it's been much more than I thought it would be when I realised who he was," he confessed.

"Anything at all you need, you've got it, Emil. Everything we've got to do can stop." I said.

"Three days, that's all it was, I could have had him you know," he said as he broke down, Luiza's arm around his shoulders.

He got something out of it though. Back at home, he told us that he went into the bar '*Cristina*' in Merano hoping to find Liebermann just sitting there. After a few beers, he began asking questions about how long the bar had been open, questions tourists would ask, the kind that wouldn't provoke suspicion. Cristina, the owner, was sat in the window watching the world pass by but overheard the conversation he was having with her daughter, Aliana, at the bar and she came over and joined them. He bought them both a drink and they sat there for an hour or so.

In mid conversation, he noticed a photograph behind the bar, it wasn't deliberately on show; it just sat at the back behind a tequila bottle. Realising it was old, he asked Cristina if she had any photographs of the time she'd opened the bar, flattering her that it would be interesting to see such a beautiful lady in her youth. She took several photographs from a draw behind the counter. Emil feigned interest but there was only one he wanted to see, the one behind the hooch. He didn't mention it because he thought it might spook the pair of them so he kept flattering her ego with kind words about her natural beauty and letting Aliana know her looks had come from her mother's side of the family. Cristina left shortly after, telling him, "A gentleman is always welcome in Bar Cristina." Emil was quite proud of that and told us, with a smile, "Once you've got it, you never lose it." Luiza walked by and shook her head, in disbelief.

It turned out it wasn't the only talent he had. After Cristina left, Aliana needed a toilet break and asked if he'd keep an eye on the bar for a short while, nobody else was in at the time so whilst she was away he took the opportunity to take the photograph. When she eventually returned, he made his excuses, telling her he might be back later that evening.

Emil handed me the photograph, "I've a good eye for faces, Eugene. It's Drexler, and is this Liebermann." He poked the picture with his finger. "And that's your man Tauber, or Wernicke as we now know him, in the background."

"It certainly is, and if you look at the man on the right almost out of the picture, it could possibly be Eichmann." Fin cut in. "The important thing is we have photographic evidence that all of them were acquainted with each other."

I smiled at the old man, he'd got lucky – something had come out of his wasted journey after all.

Luiza came in and said, "Ok, you three, conversations over. Emil is going to bed now, he really needs some sleep."

The next few days were a hive of activity. Like previously, I thought the best plan of action was to work backwards from the last known location of Mengele. Diadema was a municipality about 10 miles from the centre of São Paulo, Brazil, and my intention was to locate the farm of the Nazi sympathizer Wolfgang Gerhard who'd aided Dr Mengele to cross the border into the country. When Gerhard returned to Germany because of a family crisis, Mengele assumed his identification, the same identity he was buried with after drowning. I'd spent several frustrating hours punching the name into the Belsen database to no avail, all that came up was information we already knew about. However, I did seize onto something interesting. Mengele had taken two boxes of specimens and records of his experiments when he fled. I hadn't known that and realised I should have, it was information I might have used when interviewing Dr Magnussen. I didn't beat myself up too badly about it because we'd gotten what we needed from her, but I thought I'd just keep it in mind, you never knew when knowledge like that could be of value.

Emil, on the other hand, had managed to find one of Mengele's dissertations entitled *'Racial-Morphological Examinations of the Anterior Portion of the Lower Jaw in Four Racial Groups'*. Not the catchiest of titles.

When he spoke, I was grateful it wasn't to me. "I want you to read this, Mr Quinn. Scrutinise every last word; it may tie into your line of investigation, your idea that Mengele, Hitler and Bormann's mandibles were connected to the Lazarus Project. See if you can find anything within the paper regarding the DNA sampling, maybe you're onto something," he'd said.

After, Fin had called in some favors from some of his South American contacts and we acquired a copy of Hans Sedlmeier's coded address book. It wasn't the most elaborate of codes and I was surprised that no one had utilised it successfully before, but then again we weren't hunting down Mengele, just trying to find where he'd been in the hope that Drexler hadn't been far behind. The name Fausto Rindón was there, as well as Drexler's *and* Héctor Tauber's, all under a header titled 'Inarguable'. It looked out of place, we had four names in the address book with what seemed a strange choice of category, still we collated what we'd found and put it all into the Belsen database.

"There's another reference in the address book – *'Rill of Death"*, Fin observed. "I've heard that before, it means something, I'm sure it does."

Emil interrupted, "I can't think what the hell it is but I've definitely heard it before, as well. Type it into the search engine and see what it comes back with," he suggested.

As Fin tapped away, Emil handed me a pot of coffee he'd been slowly filling his cup with whilst thinking.

"It's an anagram of Adolf Hitler," Fin came back with. "Okay now throw in... what was it? Inarguably?"

"Inarguable," Fin corrected him, whilst typing. "Well, you've almost got an exact match for Geli Raubal, it's a letter short. There's no 'N' in her name. It's the top hit though and seeing as Sedlmeier's coding is relatively simple, I figure they just threw the letter in there to make the word complete."

"Well, I suggest we have a name then, gentlemen. Geli Raubal has been placed within this coded address book purposely. Why is the next question?

Suddenly, Fin called out, "You've gotta be shitting me!"

Luiza's voice came from the kitchen, "Language, Fin!"

"Sorry, Luiza! Guys, take a look at the names under the Rill of Death page."

We both closed in and looked at the computer screen. "It's the list of our disciples," Fin said. "So I'm thinking, let's surmise that the Lazarus Project was set up to clone DNA or re-animate life in a way that utilised the samples previously taken. We now have two lists, the one we are working on and the other headed by what seems to be an anagram of Geli Raubal."

"Ok, let's think about this," Emil said. "Mr Quinn has identified that Hitler believed himself a Messiah of some sort. It seems he believed in the resurrection and it looks like that's what he was planning. So, are we looking at a twelfth disciple in the other folder headed Geli Raubal, is she, as was suggested a few weeks back, our Mary Magdalene figure and was Hitler planning to re-animate himself along with Raubal? It's starting to look that way, but why all the cloak and dagger stuff and where did they get Raubal's DNA samples from?"

"There are no records we know about of Raubal's blood ever being taken, that's not to say Hitler didn't instruct the coroner to take such a sample," Fin added.

Something occurred to me. "When do we have a date of the conception of the Lazarus Project?" I asked.

Emil answered. "Simply put, Eugene, we don't, but realistically it could only have operated in a time when the concentration camps were operational, surely. Dachau was the first of such places, opening in 1933 but the Nuremberg Laws only came into effect in 1935, only then would it have been feasible for such a project to flourish." "When did Geli Raubal die?" I asked. "1931," Emil quickly replied.

The thoughts in my head were racing all over the place so I grabbed one as it scuttled past. "Wait a minute. I did a lot of reading about this, most of which went over my head, I have to say, but I distinctly remember finding out that DNA was first discovered in the mid to late 19th century but its significance in respect of determining genetic inheritance wasn't demonstrated until 1943."

Fin had been bashing about on the keyboard. "Jeez, guys. The German connection is all over this stuff." He began reading out loud *'In 1943, German embryologist Theodor Boveri provided the first evidence that the chromosomes within egg and sperm cells are linked to inherited characteristics.'*

I needed to call someone. "Hi, Jody, are you okay? We're a thinking that maybe Geli Raubal, who died in 1931, was part of the project to re-animate life, sounds crazy but stay with me. Her DNA may have been extracted in or around 1935, perhaps a little later. Is that a possibility?"

"Hi. Gene. What a way to greet a girl, but to answer your question, yes. We've spoken about this before – remember you asked me about Martin Bormann? *His* DNA was extracted many years later than you're suggesting Raubal's was. DNA has a half-life of precisely 521 years, that's to say it would take several million years for every single base pair to be completely gone. Have you not seen Jurassic Park, Eugene?"

"Wait a minute, if the half life is 521 years that only adds up to just over a thousand years?"

"Gene, sweetheart, it doesn't work that way. I could explain it to you but somehow I don't even think a drawing would help this time, not even if I used crayons."

"Does that mean you're not backing my application to join Mensa?"

"Gene, I love you very much. You're a great detective but a lousy scientist."

"Gee, honey, I appreciate that and I'll take your answer as a yes then, thanks for your help and I'll see you later. If you've no plans, maybe, we'll eat out, my treat. Ok? Great! Love you too." I looked at my colleagues. "She says yes, it's more than possible."

Emil pondered on the matter. "I'm sure you've both thought of this by now, but it would seem that the idea of 'reincarnation' had occurred to Hitler and his cronies much earlier than we first thought."

With that confirmed, we moved forward. We now knew that what Fin had been investigating was a possibility. Proving it wouldn't be easy though, in fact it would be nigh on impossible but we took it as part of the puzzle we were trying to solve.

We had a layout of events we believed had taken place fifty years ago or so and believed that Hitler's plans were to progress the re-animation of life in some form or another. It was strange to think that the man known to care so little for life had spent so much of his energy on projects such as this, maybe that was partly down to his feelings of guilt about Geli Raubal.

Another call from Juan Tauber, informing us his father had admitted being an overseer of the Lazarus project, not just a member of the research team. This we weren't expecting, clearly his conscience had played a part in finally admitting the role he played. We'd accepted what he'd told us and hadn't realised how vital he'd had been to the programme. I had to admit I was beginning to think he hadn't been entirely upfront with us and if I was starting to lean that way, I'm sure Fin had already fallen over but chose not to push the matter with me. We'd probably need to reinterview him, it was looking like he knew something more but now he was openly talking with his son we put it on a back burner and waited to see what else Juan came up with.

We decided that a visit to Sao Paulo was in order but a note I'd found about Dr Werner Haase, Hitler's personal physician, had led me to put a post it note on my computer; I'd planned following that up at some point but hadn't. Waiting for Fin to arrive at Emil's before we left for the airport gave me a little time to do just that. I checked the reference, a book title and website and hit the internet. Within thirty minutes, I'd read that the author had interviewed many German prisoners returning from incarceration in the USSR and one claimed he was acquainted with Haase from way back and had found himself in the same block as him, in a Gulag in some god forsaken place. This officer claimed Haase, who had the tuberculosis that eventually killed him, had discussed several matters with him, one of which was that blood was taken from Hitler in the last days of the fall of Berlin. The most interesting thing was that Hasse had apparently told him that whilst he didn't take the sample himself, he supervised a specialist who was flown in for the occasion. We'd obtained corroboration, of sorts, regarding the Bunker security log that named a Dr Lexer.

At the airport, I could see Fin's expression as we boarded the flight. I felt sorry for the guy but he never once complained openly, he just got on with the job in hand, controlled his fear of flying and kept himself to himself. Sitting at the front of the aircraft, he got off first. I sat back and allowed the melee to calm and walked off the plane not much later.

Emil had booked us into the Bela Vista Hotel, the accommodation was fantastic. It had a swimming pool, gym, restaurant and bar, the last two we made use of, the others a luxury we didn't have time for.

On the first night, we planned our schedule and a hire car was delivered at reception at seven the next morning. We headed to Bertioga, the scene of Mengele's drowning. Fin insisted on driving and grabbed the keys before me. I was a dreadful passenger but Jody had gotten used to me doing all our driving because of it. For some reason, I got motion sickness when someone else was driving. She'd told me to look out the window, 'stare at something static in the distance' and to always be part of the movement of the car. I kept those words in mind as we headed off, an almost two hour drive with one enforced stop for me to gather myself together with a bottle of water.

I'd read a Dorling Kindersley travel guide about Brazil on the flight, I thought it would kill some time on the journey and found out a little bit of information about the town we were visiting. Bertioga's number one claim to fame was it was the place where Mengele had drowned. Its top attraction was Sao Lourenco beach; in its top ten listings, nine were beaches.

Heading towards highway 101, I noticed a car tailing us from a distance. It looked like the Federal Highway Police and I mentioned to Fin to slow down, we didn't want to gain any unwanted attention but it was too late; the blues and reds came on and we were pulled over. Ordinarily, we wouldn't be too concerned but our current activities made us sensitive to the possibility of police corruption and interference from a third party.

"Leave this to me gentlemen," Emil insisted.

Strongly built with dark hair tucked under a beret, the driver approached us; badge over shirt pocket, heavily laden utility belt wrapped around khaki trousers.

After he realised we were American, he repeated his question in English. "Please, sir, step out of the vehicle."

Fin nodded in agreement and, as he complied, Emil stood out of the vehicle pretending to stretch his legs and take some fresh air.

"It's hot," he said, gesturing towards the patrolman and waving his hand in front of his face.

"Sim," replied the officer. "Tourists?" he questioned.

Emil responded, "It's my fault officer, my boys want to take me to Bertioga. I suffer from diabetes; I need to get some sugar in me. My boy, Fin here, was worried."

"I'm patrolman Gabriel. Do you need some chocolate? My companion, Carlos, he eats too much of it, he's getting a little fat around the waistline, please wait here," he said and then walked back to the vehicle emblazoned with the letters 'PRF'.

After a quick exchange of words, his colleague looked towards us and passed over a chocolate bar. On his return, Gabriel said, "Please eat."

Emil devoured it in two bites. "Thank you so much," he mumbled as he swallowed then turned towards the police vehicle, gesturing his gratitude towards Carlos. His play acting had taken the edge off our situation.

"Please slow down. I won't issue a ticket on this occasion, and please have a nice day," he offered then returned to his patrol car.

"I think we'll allow Eugene to drive on the way back, Mr Quinn," Emil said. The officers drove past us with a wave. We took a turning on the left towards Bertioga, heading down an avenue laden with palm trees, the people walked slowly, drained of life from the hard beating mid-day sunshine. The pavements were made from small mosaic pieces and I wondered how long it had taken to put down.

We booked into our accommodation and it was then Emil told us he'd arranged a meeting. When we asked who with he just said, "You'll see."

We met at another hotel, the Riviera de São Lourenço, which backed onto the beach. Its seafood restaurant grabbed my attention, I hadn't eaten since breakfast and I could feel my insides craving food.

The man held a hand out towards Emil and then in turn did likewise to Fin and me. "Hello, I'm Francisco Collor, welcome to Bertioga. Shall we take a seat and order some coffee?" he suggested.

"Can I order some food?" I asked of no one in particular. "That's a good idea, Eugene. None of us have eaten properly today. Shall I get a menu?" Emil suggested.

As we waited for our drinks to arrive, Emil told us our new friend was a well respected local historian and he hoped he would be able to provide us with some relevant knowledge of the area. Francisco began telling us a little about himself, how he'd gotten into the history of the town of Bertioga in particular. "I was born a few miles from here but as a student I travelled. I spent many years in America, where I learned the language. When I was thirty my mother took ill and I returned to take care of her, supposedly for a short while but I never went back to America. Her illness lasted a lot longer than was anticipated and she finally succumbed to it. I never really had the heart to leave my hometown after that. I work in the central library in Santos which is where my interest grew about the history of my town. As a child I hadn't been made aware of its 'notoriety'." He chuckled at the thought. "I suppose the locals of the village didn't want to talk openly of such a thing, I found it interesting though."

Shortly after, the meals arrived and the conversation became more generalized, where he'd been on his travels, were we happy with our hotel, etc.

When we'd finished, Francisco said, "Mr Janowitz, you told me over the telephone that you were interested in

Dr Mengele. I can tell you all that is known but I sense there's something more you seek, would I be right in assuming that?"

"I'm looking for a man who doesn't exist, Francisco. He doesn't appear in any records, in fact we believe we hold the only known written evidence of his life within our files, but you just might know something that could assist us," Emil replied.

I interjected. "Francisco, are there any little out of the way places in this region, somewhere you could go into hiding from the rest of the world possibly?"

"Mr Kennedy, this area is surrounded with possibilities for such a thing. It's the reason why Mengele and others chose this area; they knew they could live generally unnoticed in such a place and its surrounding dense forests. My answer to you, therefore, is yes, it would be very possible."

Emil waved a waiter over and asked for his pen. Scribbling something down, he handed it back and slid a serviette across the table to Collor. "Francisco, I'd like to employ you for several weeks and I'm assured you have no agenda. Mr Quinn here has checked you out. Would that be acceptable to you? As you see, I pay very well," he said, which surprised Fin and me as my partner most certainly had not checked him out.

Collor opened the folded napkin, his eyebrows rising slightly. "I don't have a problem with that, Mr Janowitz. It's very generous. I have time on my hands at the moment. The places we discussed over the telephone, I can show you, but for this money I have to wonder what else I can do."

Chapter 9

Francisco Koeller

Back at our hotel, I asked Emil how he'd found Collor and why he'd said Fin had checked him out when we all knew he hadn't.

"It was a happy coincidence, Eugene. I contacted the University in Sao Paolo trying to find someone with a good knowledge of the region and a professor there suggested I could do no better than Francisco. He said he had an eidetic memory but the odd thing was he didn't seem to recognise that fact himself." He hesitated. "When we took that stroll through the town, did you notice how much detail he provided when I asked about the streets we were walking down? Intricate details, as if they happened only yesterday. Why did I say he'd been checked out? I wanted him to believe we have more influence than we probably have. I've done my research, Mr Kennedy. All will be revealed soon."

He accepted a cold drink from the waiter as we sat on the terrace overlooking the pool then continued. "I've dealt with people like him before. I was involved in a case way back, a serial killer. This guy killed 93 people over a period of 35 years and what stood out was he'd go into intricate detail of the crimes he'd committed as if the decades hadn't existed. He'd see things in his mind like he was reading a book or describing a photograph. I think Francisco has the exact same trait."

"So, how are you going to harness this ability?"

"Maybe we could start with showing him the photographs of Drexler and see what he comes up with," he replied with a smile.

We'd arranged to meet Francisco at our hotel the following day. Emil had recently bought a Macintosh PowerBook which was quite a piece of equipment. It could connect to the internet with just a few clicks of the mouse and you'd hear a dial up tone that would connect us to our database back at Idar Court, we could now utilise it anywhere in the world. Francisco entered the suite, greeting us with a smile.

"How can I be of assistance to you gentlemen," he said, tentatively. Emil sat him down at the computer and acquainted him with some details of our work, explaining about the Die Spinne network amongst other things. He told him about the blood samples and the possibility of DNA being extracted, it was at that point Francisco stopped reading the screen in front of him and looked up to Emil.

"Really, they did that," he said with curiosity.

"I'm afraid so. We've uncovered something that revolves around that and we have to get to the bottom of it," Emil said, encouragingly, patting him on the back and feeding him more and more information. I worried he was saying too much, but it was his case, he had the overall say on what was divulged.

When Emil spoke of the red clay that had been found on Bormann's skull, Francisco said, "We have red clay around these parts. In fact, I can show you if you like?"

Outside the restaurant, he walked towards the growing border plants. "These are Tibouchina Urvilleana, we call them the Princess Flower; they grow best in acidic and well drained soils. This is a particular problem in these parts. Now watch if I dig a little underneath the plant," he said, using his bare hands to shovel away the dirt until he got about half a foot under.

"You see here, at this level, there are small fragments of clay, it's caused by disturbing the earth, the clay underneath is solid; we've only scratched the surface. The description in your report has the same pigmentation as what you find here," Francisco showed us a handful of dirt. "It may be coincidence, I'm sure there are many areas in this hemisphere that have this clay, not just Paraguay."

When we'd returned to the suite, he was shown the Drexler photos and gave the response, "You have photographs of a man called Jacob Altman in those files, I just saw them. You've interviewed him."

"How do you know his name, Francisco? There's nothing we've shown you to disclose it. Where have you read it?" Emil asked our local historian.

"His name appeared under a photograph in a national newspaper. It was taken at the beginning of the 1970s, an alleged sighting of Bormann going by the name of Ricardo Bauer. It was taken on the Argentine border and later discredited," Francisco replied.

"Interesting," Emil mused, "In what particular way was his name connected to the photograph?" he asked.

"As a Nazi hunter. He was in the background, just like he is on these pictures you have. It'll be on the internet, let's see if we can pull it up," he said, turning to the monitor, and a short while later, we were looking at the archived article.

Francisco volunteered: "Altman's interest at that time was, of course, Bormann and Mengele. The rumours were that this man in the foreground was Bormann but it wasn't. The picture was taken by an associate of Altman."

Emil was silent for a few moments then said, "How do you spell your surname? Do you spell it C-O-L-L-O-R or perhaps another way, like K-O-E-L-L-E-R?"

Francisco just stared at him as if caught in the headlights.

"In Sao Paulo," Emil continued, "there was a man who spelled his name the second way. A qualified German dentist who never practiced in Brazil, yet he'd been an Odontologist in Germany. He was discovered in a pool of blood, in his home, a cheap gun by his side. With no signs of a break in, a half used bottle of anti-depressants found in the bathroom, the Police concluded it was suicide. But you suspected it wasn't, didn't you, Francisco?"

He visibly sagged in the chair and simply said, "Yes."

"It's common practice to change your name to avoid being associated with a certain element of the 'German' community," Emil said to the room, as Francisco slouched back in his chair. "What was your father involved in?"

He released a sigh and said, "He was working for a man who would visit him from time to time. I saw him on several occasions when I was a boy. He never came alone, one or two other men with him, younger men. It struck me they were there as his protection in some way. They'd arrive in an old Mercedes, he would be sat in the back and they in the front. I never really took too much notice. My father told me the work he was doing was scientific in some way but there was always various jawbones lying on the benches in his workshop at the rear of our home."

Emil sat down next to him. "What did you do when you went to the States? You said you travelled when you were a student. What did you study?"

"Dentistry. I qualified as an Odontologist."

"That would be in Boston, I presume?"

"Yes, how do you know?"

"Your English has hints of Bostonian in it. You don't get that from a simple visit. Where did you practice?"

"Denver."

"Was it your father's work that led you to that?"

"Yes, it seemed natural."

"What happened after your father's death?"

"When my father died, I had to accept what they told me but I couldn't continue in the USA because my mother needed a lot of care. She was bedridden and, without my father, she had no one and very little money. She also had dementia which was progressing. One night, not long before she died, she had a few hours of lucidity during which, in answer to my questions, she told me who the man was who visited my father. She said he was called Drexler and he was a bad man. She also told me that Papa had said to her that he wouldn't do something for them because it was unethical and that he was going to tell them that he refused."

I cut in. "Did she tell you what it was that he thought was unethical?"

Francisco shook his head. "No, she told me he never said, I asked her that very same question."

Emil gave me a glance that said 'don't interrupt again'. "Go on, Francisco, did she tell you anything more?" he encouraged.

Francisco nodded. "Only that, the night my father died, Drexler and someone else came to the house. She recognised his voice. She didn't see them from her bed but she was adamant she heard them downstairs in the hall. She said my father was surprised to see them. She must have fallen asleep because she heard nothing more."

"Who found your father's body?"

"A customer found him." He saw the enquiry on our faces and explained. "He did some charitable work from a portion of his workshop separated from the rest. It was unlicensed dentistry."

Emil smiled and put his hand on Francisco's shoulder. "Why didn't you tell us this straight away?"

"Like you, I needed to assess what I was dealing with."

Then he dropped a bombshell. Composure regained, he simply said, "The photograph of the man going by the name of Ricardo Bauer, I never believed it was Bormann because I knew it was Drexler."

"Are you sure?" Fin asked.

"The last time I saw that man was the same year the photograph was taken. Of course I'm sure."

Emil's reaction was to simply get up and pour himself a coffee, offering one to Francisco who declined. He paced the room briefly as we all watched in silence, then he said, "So my friend, the question I want to ask you now is how you knew I'd had contact with Jacob Altman? That information is unknown outside our files and you've seen nothing in what we've shown you."

"I read of Altman in a magazine. He was reported as the 'new Nazi hunter on the block'.

"I remembered the photograph and article from the early '70s. I managed to make contact with him. He didn't know anything about Drexler. At the time his associate caught him on camera they both believed Ricardo Bauer to be genuine. The local police checked his documents and declared it so. He did know it definitely wasn't Bormann. When I last spoke to him, about your contact with me, he explained your relationship. He is a loyal man, Mr Janowitz."

"Yes, Jacob and I know each other pretty well. I'd class him as a friend."

Fin and I had never heard Emil mention the guy so we were, naturally, curious. It must have been written all over our faces because Emil turned to us and said, "He was secretly known at Auschwitz as 'Jacob the Revealer'. He would tell people on the ramp to find themselves a trade. If needs be, he'd suggest one he knew was being sought." He returned his gaze to Francisco. "But he's never mentioned you."

Then he changed the subject. "So, you think you're close to finding Drexler, can you expand your reasoning to me? I understand you want to find him but we have people we can depend upon to extract him from Brazil to stand trial in a court of law that can't be corrupted. I very much doubt you could do that. I'm surmising your intent was to kill the man?"

"Yes, that's true. I know the kind of people who look after men like Drexler, they'll do anything to protect him. You should be very aware of this."

Fin stepped into the conversation. "We've been successful in some of our cases, in others another outcome was favoured, but that's decided at the time. You can never underestimate a Nazi, they're like rats fleeing a sinking ship – they'll do anything to escape justice, Mr Koeller. But, you're a little one man band and from what I hear you've no appropriate training, yet here you are on your own risking your life in the name of justice for your father. It's a mystery to me why you would do such a thing, seeing as he was working with them, which brings me to a point. Why was he working with them in the first place? Did they have a hold over him or was he yet another ardent Nazi?"

"He was never a Nazi. He was my father, Mr Quinn. But, yes, they held something over him, something from the camp. They used him to remove gold from the dead and he stole some of it. He told me it was the most desperate of times and he succumbed to self survival.

He stole to survive, lots of people committed terrible crimes to last longer than the next man. Many years ago, I judged him. One day, I stopped and tried walking in his shoes – it's a walk nobody should ever be made to take.

"Under normal circumstances, they would have shot him for stealing what was now SS gold. He told me he was actually on his knees looking at the dirt for what he thought would be his last moment but, when the SS man stood behind him, someone of a higher rank intervened. He didn't know who that was, he never saw him because he was dragged away and given to Mengele who used him on a special project involving dentistry and forensic techniques. All he knew was what they told him to do, examine teeth and jawbones, take samples. He said they called it 'Lazarus'. So, do you still not understand why I contemplate finding this man, Drexler, and killing him?"

We looked at each other and shrugged acceptance. It seemed a reasonable answer.

Emil led off. "Ok, Francisco, where did your enquiries get you?"

"I have to be honest, not very far. The state of the Mercedes, whenever I'd seen it, told me they probably had a house in the hills, up a forest track. By the time I'd located the place it was obvious it had been abandoned for quite some time. I took a look around; they'd had some kind of laboratory up there, in the cellar." He hesitated. "They had a room down there that had iron rings fixed into the wall."

"Did you find out anything else? Where they'd gone, perhaps?" I asked.

He shook his head. "What people I could find who lived in the same area were few and far between. They knew what they were and had very little to do with them. The place was purpose built though. They told me that. It seems the Germans bussed in the workforce from other parts of the country. The whole place gave me the creeps. I don't think it was pure coincidence that Mengele chose Bertioga for a 'holiday'."

"Did you make any other enquiries?" Emil asked him.

"I tried but after I was followed several times I decided to stop. It was many months later I made contact with Jacob Altman."

"Are you willing to take us there?"

With a look of reluctance, Francisco replied, "If you really want me to, Mr Janowitz."

Emil gave him a rueful smile. "Yes, Francisco, I really want you to take us there. And, please, stop calling me Mr Janowitz, you're on the team now. My name is Emil."

Just over two hours out of Bertioga, up in the hills, we stood inside the decaying shell of what had once been Hugo Drexler's and wondered if Mengele had been there too. Francisco wasn't happy but he took us down into the cellar. There were indeed the remnants of a laboratory there, broken glass crackled under our feet and dirty empty folders labelled 'No 3' and the like lay on work tops and the floor. There wasn't much to see, they'd basically stripped the place quite efficiently. The small room at the end of the corridor with the wall sunk iron rings and pair of manacles thrown in a corner caused Emil and Francisco to leave. Fin and I lingered, noting the marks on the wall where someone had clawed away at it. We could only guess what they'd been suffering. Back in the corridor, we hesitated a while, instinctively knowing we were both trying desperately to maintain professional composure. Fin looked me in the eye and said, "You ready now?" I replied, "Yep, you?" He nodded.

We dropped Francisco off and went straight to the hotel. We wanted to hit the bar but agreed we needed to get a shower first. The place hadn't smelt bad but it hadn't smelled good and it clung to us. I hung my clothes on a dryer on my balcony.

I got to the bar in time to see Fin take a call on his cell phone. When he came back from the terrace, the news wasn't good.

"That was Kleinman. He's been working from home and he's just discovered that when he opened the 'Rill of Death' folder something in there infected his email and has been sending warning messages out. He's only just realised. At the moment, he doesn't know who they were sent to because they were sent through several different servers. He's still working on it." He picked his beer up and added, "That's possibly how Liebermann caught wind of you, Emil."

Later that evening, we sat in Emil's suite and brought ourselves up to date. It was becoming apparent that what I'd considered to be just a crazy notion of Fin's now had some merit. From everything we'd researched it appeared teeth and bones were frequently the only sources of DNA available for identification of degraded or fragmented human remains. Should the teeth be extensively destroyed bone is considered the next best site for DNA analysis and the mandible, easily disassembled from the skull, was the favoured item of use, it being the largest, strongest and densest cortical bone.

In the years between 1930 and 1945, the Nazis had obviously known this so the idea that they actually ran in conjunction with 'Lazarus' a programme to locate the graves of people they considered important to a new order, remove their jawbones, replace them with another's and extract the DNA from the original now looked like a probable intention. Unless any later autopsy was very thorough, the switch would probably go unnoticed especially if the original dental features were replicated in the replacement. Any anomalies would just become yet another mystery of life.

The Russians had custody of Hitler's remains and had destroyed them except for the cranium and the jawbone. After the cessation of the Cold War, they allowed several western scientists limited access. We theorised whether the dental work on Hitler's teeth, claimed by some to have been done after 1945, could have been part of this Lazarus associated programme. Had they somehow managed to swap the mandible, replacing it with one possibly engineered by Francisco's father? It sounded worthy of a James Bond plot but we concluded it was more likely to have been simple human error, some Russian charged with preserving the remains somehow lost the jawbone so replaced it with another rather than admit their incompetence and be sent to a Gulag in Siberia.

Given the description of his workshop, it was clear to us that Francisco's father had been involved in the whole thing but we could only speculate as to what it was that even he thought was unethical, a decision which we believed cost him his life.

In the meantime, we now had it confirmed via our new colleague, that Drexler had used an alias previously thought to be Martin Bormann's. It occurred to us that if Drexler had used the Bauer alias, attributed to Bormann by Simon Wiesenthal, that perhaps others had used it too, thereby fuelling the multitude of Bormann sightings across the world but especially in South America. Maybe we should be investigating the locations of those sightings as well as following the Mengele trail? The problem was we'd be stretching ourselves very thin and something was bound to give.

Chapter 10

The Nazi Worldview

Over the next few days, Francisco guided us to several locations that had been subject of Bormann sightings. It became obvious from speaking to the right local people that the Ricardo Bauer they'd seen had not been the same man others had seen somewhere else. The descriptions had been too diverse, you could lose weight in a month but we failed to see how someone could lose a foot in height.

Having exhausted all we could do in the region, at least for the time being, we headed for home.

Standing in the kitchen, at Idar Court, we discussed a few issues surrounding the 'science of eugenics'.

The Nazi's Eugenics programme related back to before they really got a firm grip on Germany. Work was being done on the idea before Hitler took control, but when he did, wealthy Nazi supporters started investing heavily into the ideology and the plans that were put in place shaped Nazi racial policies. It was Hitler's vision of the future, known as *the Nazi Worldview*.

"I just can't believe so many people actually believed such crap," I said. "Remember I said to you, Emil, I'd read about people being deemed 'unworthy of life' and how the words alone had chilled me to the core."

"I know, Eugene, and I was one of those people, along with other prisoners within Auschwitz and the other camps. It didn't stop there though, it went beyond race. Dissidents, political opponents and people with congenital cognitive and physical disabilities were rounded up and murdered, not forgetting the poor souls who they considered degenerates or deviants or simply labelled as feeble-minded. They wanted to rid the world of impurity they believed weaker than their own idealised Aryan race," he commented. "It seemed the world stood by watching as it happened and it turned its back on us. Even the Pope, Pius XI, detached himself of any plans to rescue or shelter any Jews at the time, he was too busy enabling Mussolini into power as the dictator of Italy," he said, with obvious disgust. "This is why I'm the way I am, the reason for my very being. Although I spent fifty years attempting to live a normal life, once you're touched by the Holocaust, it becomes a part of you. I'm sure you feel the same way, Eugene, such is the power it has on a person. Its memories should never be forgotten. I'm proud of you and Mr. Quinn, your passion for justice is evident in everything you do. I do this for my family and you do this for me," he waved away my intended protest. "But *we* also do it for all the souls lost to the Holocaust that didn't get to see their own justice, each one a person in their own right, people who meant something to somebody," he said passionately, just as the little bird skipped in through the open window and landed on the worktop next to the sink.

I looked over wondering why he was there, when I turned back to tell Emil, I saw he was squeezing his fist tightly against his chest and gasping for air, his face became distorted with pain and his eyes became fixed on me.

All he said was "Not now Filip, I have too much to do" then collapsed to the floor. My first reaction was to call out, "Fin! FIN!!"

I knelt down and checked his airway and pulse. I couldn't detect anything. I think I stopped thinking and went into automatic, the first aid training I'd taken over years in the police kicked in, two quick breaths and I started pumping his chest.

Fin was at the door in seconds. "Call the paramedics, Fin!! I think he's had a heart attack!" I shouted.

Another breath, or two, I can't remember. "Come on Emil you can do this," I encouraged as I started to count another 15 chest compressions.

And so it went on for what seemed an age. The sweat began to pour off me and my arms were getting tired. Fin took over whilst I slumped against the kitchen cabinets getting my breath back. I was ready to take over when Fin tired but he didn't, he just kept on going. The next thing I remember clearly was the paramedics bowling in and taking over, seems Fin had the foresight to open the front door whilst he was calling them.

"The little bird chirped happily, which gave me a feeling of calmness, his beautiful trill put me at ease, I didn't know where I was but it felt welcoming. I began to walk towards a bright light ahead of me that seemed to have shadows of people in amongst it. I could hear someone calling 'Emil!' As I continued almost floating

towards the shapes and the noise colour became noticeable, it grew brighter and brighter until I saw the shape of a person wearing a red dress, a child... it's Anna! Little Anna. She smiled, 'I've missed you so much,' she said. I stroked her hair 'Oh, little one what did they do to you!'

She smiled again. 'It's alright, mama was with me, it only hurt for a little while, I'm at peace now,' she told me. A pounding sound echoed from the walls that seemed to closely surround me. 'You must find mama now, Anna. Is she close by?' I asked. 'She's right by your side.'

As I turned, my mother stood beside me, the same age she'd been the last time I'd seen her, over fifty years ago. 'I knew you'd tell your story, you're a good boy,' she told me as tears began to fall. 'I love you so much, mama. I've missed you for such a long time,' I told her, my weeping now blurring my vision.

A voice from behind – 'Your work isn't complete yet.' 'Papa! Oh god!' I cried, grabbing hold of him tightly. 'Please forgive me,' I begged. 'I'm so sorry we couldn't help you.'

'You did what I asked of you,' he smiled. 'Filip found us, see,' he pointed towards the end of the corridor we stood in, I could see a shadow in the darkness but I knew it was Filip. I ran immediately towards him but the walls closed in on me. 'Filip, Filip!' I shouted as a blinding light hit me.

Fin and I sat in the waiting room, not knowing what to say to one other. Drexler was irrelevant now, we just wanted our friend back. I'd phoned Luiza first and then Jody, informing them of what had happened and where we were. Luiza arrived first and was tearful but relatively composed apart from an underlying current of anger with Emil for ignoring her and pushing himself too hard. When Jody arrived she took Luiza under her wing, she could tell we didn't quite know what to do with her.

It was a difficult time for us all, I hadn't realised how much the old man had meant to me, as awkward as it was to say, he'd become a father figure to me, I don't know why. After my first visit to the intensive care unit I was shocked to see a machine doing Emil's breathing for him, they'd placed him under coma conditions for observation, to see if his brain had sustained any long term damage. After a few days, he came round. As we walked into his room, he smiled. "I'm sorry. I've caused you all a lot of trouble. Luiza why are you here? Who's looking after Max?"

"Emil Janowitz, don't you dare be giving me a hard time! Max is fine. The kids are taking turns with him." She held his hand and gave him a long kiss, so long Fin and I were getting slightly embarrassed.

"They tell me I had a heart attack. Non myocardial infarction they called it. The Doctors are very good in here. I'm on clot busters but I don't have high blood pressure, in fact they tell me for a man of my age I'm quite healthy," he laughed, which made Luiza cry.

"You work too hard for a man of your age, I understand why you do it, but it's got to stop. These two will do more, won't you, boys?" she said. We mumbled stuff and nodded our heads almost violently.

Emil interrupted her, gently. "I saw my family, Luiza," he said lifting her chin with his hand whilst smiling at her. "What," she asked, incredulously.

"I saw them, they're fine. I even saw Filip at a distance." He suddenly looked at me with a strange look on his face but then recognition must have crept in, "Yes, I saw him, he saved me I think." His eyes filled with tears not wanting to fall.

When Emil returned home he had to take it easy and over the next months he started to regain his health. He didn't let up on us though; the telephone became his constant companion. Francisco remained in Bertioga, but because Emil had taken a liking to him, he kept him on in an advisory role and eventually we'd return to the town, but for now, we had to bide our time until Emil was fit enough to oversee the operation we'd yet to plan. In the meantime, we chased various dead-ends and followed leads that led nowhere, all of which we couldn't have done before.

Slowly, with the help of his pal Max and Luiza fussing over him, Emil regained strength. Taking walks with the dog through Greenwich Common helped build his up stamina, so much so that after only a couple of weeks he entered the study and began assisting one day. I mentioned about taking it slowly but he waved his hand dismissively, it was only when Luiza entered the room with two cups of coffee and a plate of sandwiches for Fin and me that the atmosphere changed.

"Oh no you don't, Mister! Get yourself back in that living room, you're not getting involved with any of this work until I can see you're one hundred per cent fit again," she scolded.

"I was just seeing how the boys were getting on, I miss working with them Luiza," he said.

"Emil, the problem is you can't just dabble at something, it's not in your nature, *you* have to throw yourself head first into things and right now, you're not well enough to do that. You're under Doctors' orders to take it easy for another month, or two if I have my way. Now get out of here, scram! You're banned!"

"I'm going stir crazy, even the dog's getting tired of walking all the time, you have to allow me something to do Luiza," he pleaded.

"Eugene, if *this* man enters the room I want you to report straight to me! I'll have him out of the living room and into the bedroom faster than quick silver," she said.

"I should be so lucky," Emil muttered under his breath.

"I heard that. Emil Janowitz! Now go!" she said pointing a finger out of the room.

Both Fin and I smiled at the timid man walking out of his own study. Like a naughty school boy, he wandered away muttering under his breath, "I remember when I used to own this house you know."

Luiza looked at us both with a stern face. "He's not well enough, boys, you know that. Help me to keep him under control. You can give him reports on how you're progressing, it will keep his mind occupied. I know he's a pain in the ass but we love him, none of us want to go through all that chaos again."

"It's not a problem, Luiza, you can trust us both. We'll look out for him. I'll pass through an update before I leave tonight, oh and by the way, you're right, he *is* a pain in the ass, but he's our pain in the ass," I confirmed to Luiza who smiled back at the both of us.

"You're good boys, both of you," she said.

Fin seemed a little uneasy at that comment, maybe his age was a reason for it, being called a boy probably made him a little uncomfortable.

With a little time on our hands, Fin and I decided to dig deeper into the eugenics programme the Nazi's had set up and focus on things that we hadn't really had the time or the inclination to do before. I discovered California formed the foundation of the Eugenics programme and it had spread to Germany by 1933. California had carried out more forced sterilizations than all the other American states combined. This I hadn't known and had been blissfully unaware of 'our' role in the programme. Dr Magnussen's words suddenly became a little clearer to me, she'd referred to eugenics as '*An idea* before it's time'. I started thinking maybe, looking at things in hindsight, we were guilty of immense prejudice but then I quickly remembered all the things Magnussen had perpetrated in the name of science and put those thoughts to one side.

Another revelation was finding out the Rockefeller Foundation had funded the Kaiser Wilhelm Institute for Anthropology. The Eugenics programme wouldn't have gotten off the ground without that assistance. Their money donated was even used to fund some of Dr

Mengele's research, which both surprised and shocked me at the same time.

Rockefeller money had encouraged Hitler to promote the belief that the German bloodstream had been infested by degenerate elements and that over time it had deteriorated so much that doing anything other than advocating the sterilisation of people who were not of pure Aryan race would be an abhorrence. He believed Germany had been burdened with people born with deformities and they should never have been allowed to live in the first place. He balanced that morality by considering the 'benefits' this would bring to the lives of healthy children. But, it would be the California compulsory sterilisation programme, which removed the capacity of certain individuals to reproduce, that would ultimately show Hitler the way forward; the beginning of his chilling master plan – the total eradication of the Jewish race from the face of the earth. Reading all of this in modern times seemed to be so out of whack, it was crazy and hard to comprehend how intelligent people of that time could have ever thought the way they did, but they did and because of that millions died.

It was around this time Jacob Altman turned up. "I heard you'd had a heart attack, old friend. You must remain strong. Are these two looking after you?" he asked, gesturing towards Fin and me.

"They're good boys, Jacob. I'm very fond of them, although I don't like saying that in their presence, they get big headed you know," he said whilst Fin and I smiled in acknowledgement.

"I understand you met my friend, Francisco," Altman continued. "He's a good man. He has memories that I wish I could take away from him, but he's not his father," That made me briefly think about Marlon Keesler, I had certainly, initially, judged him on the basis of who his father was but now I wasn't sure about him.

Fin and I left them to talk amongst themselves, I was sure they'd have a lot to catch up on.

Returning to my reading about eugenics, the law the Nazis put in place had advocated procedures for denunciation and evaluation of people and I found it repugnant that people actually turned their own neighbours or family members in for sterilisation or worse. I sat contemplating what the Nazi's had created and put into practice, encouraging the population to secretly denounce someone they were likely to have known. Do you just then go about your business like nothing's happened? I found it immoral, but it was a law used often, many people were not only sterilised but also euthanized because the Nazi's believed them unworthy of life. People were sat in front a Genetic Health Court and their lives were decided by strangers and the speed was frighteningly fast. Some might say, 'Hitler had formulated his ideals and with power he enacted his will upon the populace', but it was a lie. Hitler and eugenics had many, many eager supporters and *no one was forced* to denounce another as suitable for sterilisation or euthanasia. They did it out of hatred, jealousy and personal gain of some sort.

The *Gesellschaft fur Rassenhygiene* or German Society for Racial Hygiene was founded in 1905. It received widespread support. Soon, branches were created in multiple cities in Germany, as well as in Sweden, the

United Kingdom, the United States, and the Netherlands. In the 1930s, over 1,000 members were included in the society. The society members advocated sterilisation and euthanasia which manifested itself in the 'Aktion T4' program which killed over 300,000 people and two of the Doctors involved were Society members *and* on our list.

It wasn't pleasant reading, but it needed to be done to get an all-round picture of the people we were dealing with, specifically what kind of human being Drexler was.

Fin read something about the Vatican having ties with an illegal Italian Masonic lodge known as P2, Propaganda Due. There wasn't much in what he was saying but it made it obvious there was a long standing link between the two and because of connections with P2 members the Institute for the Works of Religion, otherwise known as the Vatican bank, was plunged into disrepute and came under heavy scrutiny in the early eighties, rumours were being touted of money laundering for the Mafia amongst other things, but I was more interested in what their role might be with the stores of Nazi gold, cash and trinkets from the murdered victims of the Holocaust and whether it tied into our operation. Could they have laundered the Nazi money? It was a possibility. Vatican representatives had aided fleeing Nazis and US Intelligence had courted them because of their anti-communist credentials *and* for the sole purpose of getting their priests to supply information from the Eastern European countries during the cold war.

Most of our work was research, we did a lot of it, but it wasn't the sum total. We had to use initiative on many occasions and, whilst Emil was in recovery, we had plenty of time on our hands. In the long term, that would prove invaluable to our investigation. Spring crept up on us and the weather brought good health to our boss and he was looking much better in himself. I joined him and Max on a walk one morning, telling him about the gates at the front of Greenwich Common, "They actually do look similar to the gates at Auschwitz," he'd agreed.

Eventually, Emil made a decision which would send Fin and me back to Bertioga; I think Luiza fanned that flame. Emil remained at home to oversee the operation, the flight would be an encumbrance to him and although able in mind his body wasn't what it used to be. With that decision made, Fin and I flew out to Sao Paulo; once there we met up with Francisco.

He informed us about a link he'd found whilst researching historical documents through the library he worked in. It concerned Wolfgang Gerhard, who we knew had returned to Austria where he died in a car accident in 1978. Francisco told us he'd given his Brazilian documents and house to Dr Mengele, we told him we knew that already but he said he believed it was an exchange of some sort. What he was saying was, there was a distinct possibility that the real Wolfgang Gerhard had acted as a courier in the disposal of whatever research files Mengele couldn't bring himself to destroy. Ok, Gerhard was dead, if he had Mengele's files, what would he have done with them? How about any surviving family members? A simple reply of 'None' had been a disappointment. For now it was yet another 'going nowhere enquiry'. As Emil had said, we were still chasing the world's most wanted war criminal yet we knew exactly where he was – buried under the name of Wolfgang Gerhard in grave number 321 in *Our Lady of the Rosary Cemetery* in the town of Embu das Artes. His later exhumation confirmed his DNA; the remains were definitely Josef Mengele.

What we were looking for was a link, any link to Drexler, something must come from all the work we'd put in. It was frustrating. "He can't have just disappeared from the face of the planet," I moaned to Fin.

We were having a few beers at Francisco's place when Kleinman called. "I've found a file I can't get into, as you know I used to do this for a living, the interesting thing here is the wall I'm trying to break through. I've only ever come across this in my hacking days, specifically when I was investigating the Pope. It's a Vatican encryption. I was looking at what they were up to back in the day, laundering mafia money, diverting US funds, that sort of thing. For this to be so heavily encrypted means they're protecting something they really wouldn't want the rest of the world to know about," he suggested. "If I ever crack it you'll be the second to know."

"Who'll be the first?" I stupidly asked.

"That'd be me, obviously." He signed off.

More food for thought but we didn't have time to mull it over too long; Francisco had something else to tell us. He sipped a Nova Schin beer then imparted, "I've been looking into modern day eugenics and it's a legitimate field of science. Individuals can, by choice rather than force, submit samples for genetic testing. An individual can't be compelled into testing or be forcibly sterilised based on results from a specific genetic test but it's tied in with what they call genome editing, the modification of genes for various purposes. Modern eugenics are called 'Newgenics', also known as 'Neo Eugenics', and that made me pay particular attention, as does anything with the word Neo before it." We laughed, knowing where he was coming from with that one. But, he continued. "I dug a little deeper and found that there's a revitalisation of the euthanasia programme in disabled new born children being considered, for me the very idea of judging the quality of a disabled child's life is tantamount to the same dogma that the Nazi's used back in the thirties. I find it frightening that this is being considered in some countries of the world today, that's what caught my eye," he explained.

"That can't be true Francisco, surely," Fin questioned. "Well, you know only too well what the Nazi's got away with. The world in general didn't know what was being done to the people within the concentration camps at the time. For me I'd rather err on the side of caution and look at the world with open eyes that understand what mankind is capable of. I hope I'm wrong but it's talked about in scientific quarters, and they obviously refer back to the Nazi Doctors of Death often. My reading of it shows a science world looking for an excuse to continue that work and put aside what happened in the Second World War as purely the work of a madman. They obviously don't want to be tarnished with the same brush as Mengele, but the reality is the same idealisms are present today as they were back then, they just paint a prettier picture. Countries such as Switzerland, Belgium, the Netherlands and several others all allow assisted dying, the reality of this is it could be the first step towards a programme that was banished after the War. People see it as the decent thing to do, which it possibly is, however you can't separate history from the facts. You've got to constantly monitor Euthanasia because of its history, or evil could easily overthrow power," he commented and I kind of understood his meaning but wasn't overly convinced with his comparison.

He wasn't finished though. "There is a company called 'D.I.D' – 'Dignity in Death'. I found it whilst researching and joined a forum where people made comments about the euthanasia programme. There are real working doctors in this group giving opinions to people who have opposing views. On one hand, the Catholic Church's stance on euthanasia is that it's a grave violation of the law of God; a deliberate and morally unacceptable killing of another human being. 'Thou shall not kill' is the fundamental principle of Catholicism and no matter how grave a situation is, it's a belief they will never waver from. On the other, if a person wants, genuinely, to end their life shouldn't they be able to do that with dignity?"

I responded, "I tend to take what the Catholic Church says with a pinch of salt, Francisco. They initiated all manner of religious wars and aided fleeing Nazi's after the biggest. I don't think we'll take any advice from them. Otherwise, I'm in complete agreement."

He smiled. "I'm not trying to convince you of anything, they were just personal observations. But here's the thing, I found something that may be of interest to you. In this particular forum, there are about two hundred people contributing to the board, one particular person caught my eye, his bulletin board name is Dr X. I read back through his extensive posts. He joined the notice board at its conception in 1991. My view of the man is that he advocates euthanasia for the disabled and, as he put it, the feeble minded people of this world. He isn't a popular person, in fact I'd go as far as to say his views were deliberately controversial, he got a lot of angry responses to some of his posts."

I didn't know where he was going with this particular observation; I couldn't see how it would be of interest to us and our activities.

He tried again to get our attention. "Dr X."

"Dr X." I parroted back.

"That's right, Eugene, I'll show you on the computer." He turned towards his monitor. "Here, this is him, he doesn't rant in his posts, he's very articulate and knowledgeable about the subject he's talking about. I believe he's worked within the field because there's certain things you just couldn't know about and he does. Some of the things he spoke of, nobody understood and they'd condemned him for what he was saying. On such occasions, his answer would be a simple, *'I just inform the truth'*. I've seen him say those words many times, but something really stood out – he once said *'In Germany, the concept of 'Eugenics' is mostly known under the term of Rassenhygiene or 'racial hygiene.'* He was talking in the present tense and yet these are words from the past. It was a red light to me and stood out from the rest of his comments, it was like he had inside knowledge of something that was happening today. With all that you've uncovered and told me about I took particular notice of Dr X, and started thinking with an investigative mind." He paused to see if we'd caught up with him. I glanced at Fin who looked as vacant as I was.

I sensed frustration in Francisco's voice when he next spoke. "Take the first four letters of Drexler's name and what have you got?"

I have to admit, by this time, Fin and I had sunk quite a few beers so the dawning came slowly. "D-R-E-X"

Fin tapped me on the leg. "Gene, I get it now. Dr EX, pal."

The light bulb in my head shone brightly. I could have happily kicked myself. "Dr X!" Before I could say more, Fin said, "This we must follow up on, I'll get Kleinman on the phone. We need this guy's physical location from that web forum."

We gave him everything he needed and within thirty minutes he called back. "I used some specialist software and I can tell you the physical address is Estrada Alvarenga 5555, Eldorado Paulista. It's a suburb of Sao Paulo."

"Jesus! That's where Mengele moved to in the mid seventies," Fin exclaimed.

"The same goddam house?" I said quietly.

Fin just nodded his head slowly and meaningfully.

Could Hugo Drexler really be living in Brazil in the same house where Josef Mengele had lived? There certainly seemed a possibility of it and we had to get feet on the ground as soon as possible.

We updated Emil. "Francisco, you're an asset to this investigation and I'd like your photographic memory onboard with this one. Will you go along with Fin and Eugene on this mission, these guys are quite accomplished and they'll look after you," he said.

"Yes, it would be an adventure, I'd love to help," he said, enthusiastically.

I looked at Fin who I knew thought the same as I did *'Do we get a say in this?'* but it was already decided. We didn't object to the guy, it was just we'd now have someone else to worry about. We could take care of ourselves but Francisco was untested. I suppose you have to start somewhere, but I just wondered, *'Why now?'* It mattered not, Francisco was on board and it would be Fin and me that would have to wet nurse him.

Later that same night, Emil spoke with Fin and me again, "Look, I know you think Francisco will be a burden to you, but I have a feeling about the man, there's something about him I like, he has a feisty spirit and I think he'll be an asset to you both. I'm sure he won't burden you either, after all, he uncovered this, so it really is his ball we're playing with," he assured us.

I wasn't overly convinced. "Emil, the thing is, this could get messy. We don't know how it's all going to play out and I don't want the responsibility of another man's life on my hands."

"Will you do it for me, Eugene?" he asked.

I turned away so as to muffle my voice from the phone. "Jesus H," I muttered under my breath. Turning back towards the receiver I gave it my best shot "Yeah, sure, Emil," I said looking at Fin who'd also surrendered to our boss's request. Emil had that over you, *and* he knew it, the son of a bitch. You just couldn't say no to him.

Chapter 11

Dr X

The next day, we organised maps, planned our journey and set off on the two hour trip to Sao Paulo and Eldorado Paulista.

Before we left, Fin took me to the trunk whilst Francisco was getting some drinks and snacks from the shop across the street.

He opened a black bag. "We've got added insurance. Taurus PT92, basically a Brazilian manufactured copy of the Beretta 92." He quickly cleared it, showing me it was empty and safe. "Three mags of 15 rounds each. Should be more than enough to suppress or allow us to extract." It was a good job I knew the terminology, Francisco would have been clueless.

"How did you get these, Fin?" I thought I knew the answer though. I was right.

"I did a lot of work in South America, Gene. You know that. Let's just say a friend helped me out."

I loaded up and put the spare mags in my jacket pocket then, this time, I *insisted* on driving.

Fin sat up front with me. Francisco sat uncomfortably in the back. Like me, Fin didn't want the responsibility but neither of us showed it, we were only looking out for his own good. Although he'd said he knew how determined such people and their protection could be, I don't think he was aware of how fluid these situations could become and just how rapidly things could deteriorate into a nightmare. Individually, we tried to get him up to scratch on the case, filling him in on what we thought he'd need to know and not telling him anything he didn't. There was no point in frightening the guy to death – that was my way of thinking anyhow. But, I think Fin was leaning a little more the other way, he had a wicked sense of humour that I didn't think was appropriate in our situation.

"I'm only fooling around with the guy, Eugene, it's a long drive, I get bored as a passenger, you should have let me drive," he said.

"Not a chance after last time. We don't want any interactions with the police." I replied, as he smiled in recollection.

Estrada Alvarenga was a long street but it wasn't too long before we found ourselves in the right area. We could find 5531 and up to 5637 but weren't surprised we couldn't quickly identify 5555 because house numbers appeared to be unpopular. The local postman must have been a Society of American Magicians fully paid up member.

Fin shook his head. "In a sane world this wouldn't be too much of a pain in the ass but these numbers don't even make sense. There are not enough entrances from the road to the houses to equate with the numbering."

This is where Francisco came to the fore. "It should not be too difficult. I read an article in the Los Angeles Times..."

"You get that here?" I cut in.

"I don't but the library has a wide selection of English speaking newspapers. This one was from 1985. It was about the where Mengele lived before he died. He stayed with the Stammer family for a long time. They used to own 5555. Later, after he died they sold it to the Bosserts, the people he was with at Bertioga, The article describes certain things. We're looking for a bungalow, possibly still painted yellow. It might still have a small building to the rear of it, Mengele fixed up a one-room caretaker's house at the back. It's also not far from the reservoir."

"I haven't seen a reservoir around here" Fin commented.

"Yes there is. I caught a glimpse of it, before through the trees. It's just over there, down in the valley."

We took a few drive-bys and couldn't get a good enough view; all the properties were walled in with a lot of vegetation. We could only make out the roofs but, even so, we thought we had two hopefuls. Fin and I discussed how we would have to do a close up recce at night, get over the wall and sneak around. We'd no idea what security they might have, although the nature of the neighbourhood suggested that it wouldn't be more technical than a dog or two. That's what worried us – it's no fun having a Rottweiler attached to your leg.

Francisco solved the issue for us. "Turn around, I'll ask that old guy sat on the bench."

After a short conversation, the old man pointed and Francisco climbed back into the car. "It's that one over there."

"What did you tell him?" I asked.

"I just asked for 5555 and he asked if we were looking for the Mengele house."

We'd identified the location, now it was time to do some research. We needed to check out the ownership of what we were now calling 'the yellow house' – even though we couldn't tell if it was still that color it had a certain ring to it. We figured the records office would be in Sao Paulo city hall, so that was the next stop.

Parked up, we sent Francisco in, seconds later he was back out, at Fin's window.

"I need some money. There'll be a fee."

"How much?"

"Two hundred should do."

We sat drinking cola and waited. Twenty minutes later, he was back at Fin's window. "Did you find what we want?"

He shook his head. "There were other people there, registering things, so I waited until they'd gone. The guy wants R$1500. That's about $300. Clearly, it's a bribe but no pay, no get. He says he'll Xerox us copies for that as well," he explained.

"Well, we need that information and I've got about R$1000 on me, what have you got, Fin?"

"I can cover the remainder," he replied.

Francisco went back in. This time, Fin discreetly tailed him to ensure we weren't being set up. Whilst away, I took a call from Emil; he'd been researching something and wanted confirmation of sightings. He said he wanted to get up to speed on what we may uncover and to arm us with as much Intel as possible. The problem was he confused the name Mengele with Bormann several times and even noticed it himself, apologising for the blunder but it worried me. He said he'd done it quite a few times that day and tried to laugh it off but I'd seen him do it on many occasions recently.

Fin returned with Francisco in tow. "This guy isn't as stupid as he looks, Eugene," he said, waving a thumb at his companion. "He knew I was following him then he negotiates the price down to R$1250. Here's the change," he said with a broad smile. "I'm warming to the kid."

"I was thinking about our funds, we have to eat guys and I noticed you seemed to have pooled all you had," the 'kid' chipped in.

In the corner booth of a fast food restaurant, we examined the documents Francisco had obtained. What we were interested in was the ownership of the 'yellow house' from its time with the Stammers to the present day.

Mengele had lived in Brazil under many guises. For a long period he lived with the Stammer family on several farm properties they owned. In interviews with the Brazilian police, and later the press, Gitta Stammer insisted that one day in 1961, the real Wolfgang Gerhard, an acquaintance of her husband's, appeared at their farmhouse with a man he introduced as a Swiss national named Peter Hochbichlet. She was told he had knowledge of farming and would be good company whilst the husband was away on business. Her husband agreed.

Within a year, Hochbichlet's behaviour was grating on her, his attitude being somewhat overbearing, he was anxious not to be photographed and was extremely curious of any visitors they had. His conduct struck her as *so* strange that she finally asked the man if he was hiding under a false name. He assured her he was not.

In 1962, according to Stammer, a visiting produce buyer left a newspaper at the farm. In the paper was a picture of Josef Mengele.

Stammer said she confronted the purported Swiss national with the picture and demanded to know if he was the same man. At first he denied it but then admitted he was.

Not long afterwards, Wolfgang Gerhard came to them with a man introduced to her only as Hans. It would be Hans who provided Mengele with the money he needed every month or two. Stammer said she was told they had to keep Mengele for a while further until other arrangements could be made. The matter dragged on for months and she stated that when she protested Gerhard told her to be very careful because 'something bad might happen to your children'. In the mid seventies, the Stammers rid themselves, so they claimed, by setting Mengele up in a bungalow they owned in a suburb of Sao Paulo – Eldorado Paulista, to be exact; 5555 Alvarenga Road. When Mengele drowned at Bertioga, his friends the Bosserts, who lived not far from him in the Sao Paulo suburb of Brooklin, bought the 'yellow house'. There was more going on there than anyone was letting on but we didn't want to get sidetracked.

All this information came not from the copies we'd obtained but from Francisco's memory of the article in the Los Angeles Times he'd read all those years ago. What the copies did was confirm the Stammers and Bosserts ownership and who bought the house when it was next sold. There had been several transactions since the Bosserts but the last recorded owner was listed as 'Guilherme Lobo'. Another alias of Drexler?

Francisco began to chuckle. "You know, I think they like to make fun of people looking for them."

"What do you mean?" I asked.

"Well, Guilherme means 'resolute protector' and you must know what 'Lobo' means?"

I obviously looked clueless because Fin nudged me in the side and said, "It means wolf, buddy."

"Am I supposed to know that? How do you know that?"

"I've worked in South America a lot, Gene. Do you ever listen to me?" he replied, laughing.

Resolute protector of the Nazi cause was the implication and as for wolf – that had been Hitler's pseudonym.

Without the pain of making other enquiries, at least we knew the building was most probably in the hands of an ardent Nazi or a sympathizer.

We stayed in the area as long as we could, but the nature of the street meant the only place we could park up at was the entrance to a gated and wire fenced property that belonged to the water company. It had a rudimentary breeze block built security hut which didn't seem to be used by anyone at the time. We got almost an hour out of it when this white shirted guy with stained pants came out of nowhere, told us we were trespassing and had to leave. He said if we didn't, he'd call the police. That was the last thing we wanted so we left, but we'd seen no one enter or leave the 'yellow house'. We headed back to the hotel in Bertioga.

A few beers in the bar later and we agreed we either needed to place one of us in the bushes opposite, to which Francisco played the 'I can't be trusted' card, *or* Fin and I had to get in the grounds and take it from there. Francisco volunteered to drive circuits of the road every so often, there being nowhere whatsoever to park without causing a tailback of traffic that would undoubtedly attract the attention of the police.

The following day, we did repeated drive-bys until we were satisfied we'd seen nothing to make us call it all off. Fin locked and loaded his PT92 and tucked it carefully into the back of his pants ready for use. I did likewise.

"Be prepared for anything coming at you, we know what these people are capable of," he warned.

Francisco left us at the side of the road and we walked past the entrance whilst eyeing it for security and the easiest way in. It took two passes then we decided to try the gate, if it was locked we'd quickly scale the wall at its lowest point. Surprisingly, the gate was open which meant whatever excuses we made if challenged would be more believable. The path up the little hill opened out to a view of the bungalow. It was still yellow, albeit a bit weather-worn

Suddenly, an old woman carrying logs appeared from the rear of the house and disappeared into it. I guesstimated she was in her seventies.

Our 'plan', if you could call it that, had been we'd get as close as possible, then do some surreptitious peering into windows and take it from there. The technical term for this was a close quarter covert recce, but *they* usually had much more stealth and planning to them. But now the reality was dawning on us – we couldn't just start looking through her windows because the sight of our ugly mugs leering in at her might just cause her to have a heart attack or start screaming the place down attracting all kinds of attention.

In addition, we still weren't sure about any dog presence although I think we were both fairly happy that if there was one with a mind to be belligerent we'd have seen and heard it by now. If we hadn't been flying by the seat of our pants before, we certainly were now.

An idea came to mind. "I'll knock on the front door on the pretence of looking for directions whilst you cover my back." I proposed.

"Now that's a plan, how come I never thought of that?" Fin replied, sarcastically.

It turned out, the woman was a nice lady called Clara. She lived at the property on her own, having had it bought for her by her son and daughter around six months ago. Fin used his Portuguese as best he could and put her at ease with a story that we were simply asking directions to the reservoir as we had a friend to meet there who'd promised us a boating trip but, if we were going to get anything meaningful, we knew we needed Francisco. In answer to our phone call, he arrived in decent time, parked on the entrance way and then proceeded to charm Clara into telling us all sorts of things about the place that would have either aroused suspicion or been impossible for us to do.

In answer to a series of subtle questions, she told us neither she nor her children had met the seller; it was all done through the lawyers. The price been lowered for a quick sale and the previous owner must have been a budding amateur chemist or scientist judging by the glass phials, Bunsen burners, Petri dishes and the like that had been left behind. It sounded like the place had been left in a bit of a state we said. No, it was all reasonably tidy, especially the main house. The little building at the back was where the seller had had their 'laboratory'. Francisco told her we'd never seen a home laboratory before and it all sounded interesting. She offered to show us it and we trooped into the rear garden. The place had been tidied up, her son and daughter had disposed of what had remained. Fin tapped my arm whilst the 'kid' engaged Clara in praise for her planting. On the tiled floor could clearly be seen the marks where we strongly suspected filing cabinets had been standing for years. We asked her about it. No, they weren't there when they took the place over. There had been some papers, document sort of things on the floor but her son had put them in a bonfire. She said, he'd thought they'd just fallen down the back of the cabinets. We apologised for disturbing her, thanked her for her interesting information and patted her portly, contented dog.

As we left, she called after us. There was a brief exchange of words and Francisco shouted back to her "Obrigado" and waved.

"What was that about?" I asked.

Fin replied, "She just said she'd remembered. A neighbour told her the man who lived here was a German and thought his name was 'Rexler'.

We all knew that was as far as we were going with this particular enquiry. Another dead end but we'd gained valuable intelligence. As far as we were concerned there was no doubt Drexler had been living there, probably using it as his own personal research facility and he'd not long left. It was also clear that he'd had help from some 'removal men', and very efficient ones at that.

We had one last thing to do. The house 'next door' had an open driveway further along the street. That told us they didn't have loose dogs of the type that would attack a visitor and that they weren't hiding away. Fin and Francisco gave them a visit. I waited in the car. When they returned they had more interesting stuff to tell. The 'Rexler' character kept himself to himself, although he wasn't averse to hellos, goodbyes and chats about the weather or the garden. He'd told them he was a retired chemist who'd worked for a well known multinational pharmaceutical company. It was time to go home. The next day, we left Francisco with a few minor back up tasks and a promise that if we had any more leads we'd make sure he was in on the action. I think he'd got a taste for it and, well, we kinda liked him a lot. He'd proven himself.

When we got back to Idar Court, the first thing Emil said to us was: "I've information about Liebermann, but you won't like it. He's offered us a deal, through Altman. He wants immunity in exchange for the exact current location of Drexler."

Chapter 12

Emil

I was woken by a kick to the stomach, Pleva did that often, it was his thing, he liked making you feel like you were worthless. He was a shadow of a man but I had to take what was dished out, I had a brother to think about who was getting more than enough attention from the collaborating Kapo and didn't deserve it *and* my papa who was looking frailer by the day. We ran to the wash house, readying ourselves for whatever Pleva had waiting for us. In normal times, Filip was a popular and well liked boy; I was so very proud he was my brother.

We were ordered to Block 10 to tidy up the mess an SS officer named Vogel had made of some poor soul. That block in particular was feared by everybody, it was known what went on inside and everyone tried to avoid it's reality, although trying wasn't always an option but you did what was possible – terror radiated from its very walls. They experimented on people inside; some said they killed children, specifically twins.

We were shown the remains and ordered to clean up. After placing the corpse on a cart outside, we returned, got down on our knees and scrubbed the floor until it was free of blood and bits of brain tissue. A hand brush and a bucket of cold water were our only implements, the blood was fresh and sticky, so new it still smelled of iron and made you feel nauseous. I noticed Filip feeling much the same and told him to swallow hard and continue the work or we'd be given a beating, and in Block 10 you never knew if it would be your last or if you'd ever get out.

Whilst we were on our knees, two children entered the room. I knew them from our block, Ayla and Bina, beautiful girls whose long blonde hair had been stolen from their heads upon entry to the camp; this was done to every entrant after the selection including those destined for the gas chamber.

I'd heard comments about the girls from others in the block, one woman said they'd somehow retained their beauty after the loss of such beautiful hair – she was right they had. The red coats and new black boots they'd entered the camp with had been taken from them and replaced by standard issue work dresses and ill-fitting shoes which they stood in as Filip and I cleansed the room. Before anybody else entered, I tried to reassure both girls that everything would be alright, a vain attempt to quell their fear; both were physically shaking. I feared for them, they'd been brought into Block 10 because Dr Mengele had a curiosity for identical twins and Ayla and Bina were perfect. I prayed they'd survive whatever he had in-store for them because there was nothing that could be done about it – if I tried to do anything not only would Filip and I be killed but others also, not just the terrified children stood in front of us. It was an impossible situation and I was overcome by a great shame that I couldn't help.

Mengele entered the room and saw us. "Raus hier!" he shouted. We understood enough German to get out as quickly as our legs could carry us. I silently wept at the thought of what may happen to those two little girls.

"He just took our blood," Bina said so innocently, later that night upon their return. "He probably wanted to protect you from the illnesses in the camp, my little darling," a woman said, soothingly.

"It hurt though," Ayla said, showing her arm where the needle had pierced her skin, a bruise had already formed because of the malnourishment we all endured. I was overjoyed they'd survived, so many hadn't before, you got used to not seeing children come back from Block 10, as horrendous as that seems. Parents would be elated upon the return of a young one, whilst others mourned; such was life if you were chosen for Block 10.

I remembered being at the ramp when the two girls first entered the camp, they held heather in their hands and I wondered why they'd kept hold of such insignificant things after such a long journey. I recalled thinking how innocent they both looked, not much older than three years of age, it made you realise the fragility of life within the barbed confines of Auschwitz – the world we lived within was hell, none of us deserved to be there. Seeing children in such an environment was disturbing, your own feeling of uselessness at not being able to help them was overwhelming. But, somehow we just accepted our fate, death also if it came. The unwritten rule in our block was simple – you took whatever was dished out to you to save the next man, woman or child and accepted your own destiny.

Pleva had it in for Filip that was for sure, he didn't like my brother for some reason. I wasn't certain if Filip understood the consequences of that or not, so I told him not to get on the wrong side of him, he wielded the power of life and death over us. That small piece of information changed my brother's attitude towards the Kapo, he obeyed the orders bawled at him and took the beatings dished out on a daily basis and did so with courage; for his father and me. He was a brave boy for one so young and I was proud of him. Courage isn't what you think it is sometimes, it disguises itself within actions, enduring awful conditions and accepting what fate throws at you to protect others. Filip had learnt how to survive, firstly in the ghetto and now Auschwitz.

I lay on the concrete slab I'd been allocated, staring at the bunk above. Eighteen slept there and to either side of me in a more than uncomfortable situation, but you took what you could; sleep was a luxury and all we had was exhaustion and they're not the same. At best, you'd rest your aching bones and what was left of your deteriorating muscles. You had to be so careful within the camp, dying was the easiest thing to do and there were plenty of ways of doing that. We'd seen so many people lose their lives in all manner of ways but Block 10 was feared the most. If I were to die, I didn't want it to be in there and I didn't want that for my brother and father either.

Many perished from illnesses brought about by being overworked. *Vernichtung durch Arbeit* the Nazi's called it – extermination through work. Such was the disdain they held for us, they would laugh amongst themselves as people died before their very eyes. I couldn't comprehend what had brought about such hatred.

My brother fought the battle to survive every day, but one particular person wanted him dead. He was brave though, braver than anyone else I'd seen in the camp which was a place full of heroes, each in their own right, not only for their own survival but for what they did for the person stood next to them. Of course, there were people that fell short, there always will be, it happens, people who weren't strong willed enough or without the right character, but in the main we were good people who were being oppressed by the system of government in charge. Unfortunately some of that regime were helped by collaborators, our own people given special privileges for doing the Nazi's dirty work. Kapos were normally people with a history of violence or criminal activity but a few were just stronger than the rest and the Nazi's liked that. It was a stain on the character of the people within the camp that a few, just a few, betrayed their own kind.

I wanted to be different than that and hoped for an opportunity to help, not only my brother but others within our block. I woke one morning to find Filip seriously ill, he'd been suffering under the strong arm of Pleva for a long time, he'd endured a lot and I knew if it continued his life would be stolen from him. The decision came quickly; I had no choice in the matter. Pleva must die. If he didn't, Filip would not last much longer.

I figured I could also ease the suffering of others by doing that one 'small' thing, sending out a signal that would perhaps help another survive the daily punishments dished out by the likes of that man. With my mind made up, I planned his execution, knowing full well the repercussions of my actions. If I was lucky, they would shoot me or hang me straight away, if not they would send me to Block 10. At that stage, I didn't care for myself anymore, my only reason for living was Filip; my mama and papa and dear little Anna were all now dead and we were alone in the world.

Killing Pleva was easy, the spade I'd used moments earlier digging the ground was enough to take the life blood from him, the energy I used hitting him came from a deep hatred that ran through my veins like a virus. As it struck his head, I knew instantly he was dead. I discarded his body in the place he belonged, in the communal latrine, pushing his head under. Afterwards, the little bird appeared, like a witness about to give testimony. Strangely, I didn't fear him as he regarded me, passing judgement on what I'd done, but I didn't feel he scorned me, he made me feel at ease, his coloration whispered 'Life' and I knew what I'd done was right, somehow it would help. I didn't know how yet but that would come in the following weeks. He was a vision, seemingly sent from heaven, and in these dark times he appeared like an angel showing me the path toward freedom, guiding me to forgiveness for the crime I'd committed, a mortal sin which I felt great shame for but knew it was either my brother or Pleva and there was no other option for me in that matter.

The two children Ayla and Bina continued to be experimented on, but somehow they always seemed to survive, like they were Mengele's favourites but that didn't mean he wouldn't kill them. Two young boys had been his favourites before Ayla and Bina Goshen, he'd treated them kindly, they even called him 'Uncle Mengele'; such was their trust. He killed one of those twins whilst the other was forced to watch, already knowing his own fate. Mengele wanted to see the boy's reaction to his brother's death under laboratory conditions. I feared for Ayla and Bina in the hands of this evil man. I could have called him a madman but that would absolve him of his crimes.

Bina was the smallest of the two twins, she weakened faster than her sister and the elders took care of her because of her frailty. Two identical children, yet one was weaker than the other, this was what Mengele and the other doctors where conducting experiments on, trying to extrapolate enough information to discover a reason why. Was Bina born weaker or had she been exposed to it? Both of these children had suffered at the hands of the Nazis but they'd also been given more than other children. Bina had developed deep set eyes, as if death was just a moment away, her bones protruded abnormally like others in the camp, even special treatment couldn't disguise her failing young body. Her mother was worse, illness had taken hold of her many days earlier and the fear was she'd succumb to it shortly. Sadly, it was to be that very night she passed away, her body consigned to a cart the following morning to join the others to be cremated. The two children were lost within their grief and powerless to do anything other than mourn silently. It was a common sight, death was a companion you got used to; you just tried not to be its friend.

Dr Mengele continued to use the children, even in the desperate state they were in; the perverse sense of reasoning seemed to be his own gratification. There was wickedness within the walls of Block 10, we watched the victims enter and, often, they would later be carried out and flung onto a pile to be collected later that day for cremation. Such was life within Auschwitz-Birkenau, the fear factory that murdered at will.

At selections, we trembled with dread, hopeful the angel of death would pass over us as it had the first born sons of Egypt. I realised what was happening to us was biblical, like I'd read in my scriptures as a child. In Romans 9:27 Isaiah cries out, *'Though the number of the sons of Israel be as the sand of the sea, only a remnant of them will be saved'*. I understood. The Nazi's were wiping us from the face of the planet.

I dreamt about the little bird, frequently. Vivid dreams, where we would fly over the camp together. He'd been there to console us at our loss when our father passed away; he gave respite from the never ending unbelievable misery that befell us. In my darkest hours, he sat as a companion, it was almost as if he was sent by an impotent God as an angel to observe and report.

When my brother died, I'd have gladly closed my eyes and never opened them again but that little creature seemed to watch over me. All was lost to me at that time, how could I live with this intolerable pain that consumed me?

All of this, I remembered as darkness enclosed me then suddenly faces appeared that seemed familiar. Names I recognized, Luiza, Lena and Daniel, but I didn't know why and confusion overtook me.

A face came close, I heard him speaking, 'Emil, it's Eugene, everything will be fine,' he said. Why had Filip called himself Eugene, it confounded me. Was I now dead and this was what it was like? Yet the bird sat to one side, scrutinizing me. I couldn't be dead, not with him here. Light bled through my irises with remarkable colours, for a moment I thought I was in the presence of God until my eyes focussed.

"Nurse!" I heard someone shout, a male voice, a worried tone. I looked to that side to see Filip wearing clothing that was strange to me. "Hello, what are you doing here? You died, Filip, am I in heaven?" I said.

"It's ok, Emil, You had a stroke. It's Eugene and look, Luiza is on the other side of you," he said.

"Eugene, that's a name in my dreams," I said.

"You must take it easy now, sir," a man in a white coat said. "Mengele!" I shouted in fear.

"No, no, Emil! This is Dr Johnson, he's been taking care of you," a woman to the right said, continuing tenderly, "Hello you. You scared the hell out of us all, we've been worried sick about you," then she began to weep. I was so confused, who were these people and where was I?

Had I died or not? The Eugene character wearing clothes I'd never seen before and the woman to my right, weeping for some unknown reason.

"I'm sorry my dear, who are you?" I asked, not wishing to upset her any further than she already was. She gave a concerned look towards the doctor in the white suit.

"It's alright, Mrs Janowitz, it can happen like this sometimes, it's quite normal for a little memory loss, a stroke can affect all kinds of things," he said to 'Mrs Janowitz'. There was a man, in a wheelchair, at the end of the bed and I wondered if he was Mr Janowitz, he looked old enough to be anyway, but then he abruptly went away. I asked about him but nobody seemed to know who I was talking about.

"There've only been three of us in the room, Emil, nobody else, you must be seeing things," 'Eugene' said.

"He was sitting in a wheelchair," I told him.

The woman turned to 'Eugene' and murmured, "He means Aleksy Markowski."

I heard her and I recognised the name, though I had no idea why. Looking closer, I realised the man calling himself Eugene wasn't Filip at all. I'd thought he was at first, but he couldn't have been, he was older, much older than my brother though he looked so familiar.

I told them both, "Thank you for coming, I don't know who you are but thank you anyway. I need to get some rest now, I feel exhausted."

"That's fine, Emil, I'll be outside. I love you old man," the woman said.

"Why do you love me?" I questioned.

"You're my husband, Emil Janowitz. I've loved you for over fifty years and I'll always love you," she told me.

"Really, I'm so sorry, I don't remember you Luiza..." yet I knew her name then I recalled someone saying it earlier but I began to cry in bewilderment of it all.

They both came to my side. "Oh, Emil," she said whilst 'Eugene' leant over me and said, "It's ok, we'll get you back to normal, I promise."

"Can you help my family? Anna's only a child and Filip, he's such a good boy. He looks like you. Can you help them?" I pleaded in my confused state.

***

Outside the room, Dr Johnson explained what was happening to Emil. "We need to keep a close eye on him, he has early signs of vascular dementia, he's having problems with his memory which although isn't good, there is a better side to this, it suggests he isn't suffering from Alzheimer's disease, but we'll run a few tests to make sure. Strokes are usually brought on by prolonged use of alcohol, tobacco or drugs, but it can also be triggered by lack of sleep, depression or stress."

Luiza interrupted. "He eats very well but he's always stressed. I've been telling him to take it easy for months but once he's on a case he won't let go," she said.

"What does he do for a living, is he a policeman?" Dr Johnson enquired.

I responded first. "He used to be a detective in Greenwich but in his retirement he was given a case file, you may have heard of it in the news. We work on historical war crimes, bringing to trial those that thought they'd got away with it," I told him.

"Are you the guys who brought down Hans Schröder?" he asked.

"That's us. Emil's the mastermind behind it all."

"Then he really must start to take his health seriously, this is a warning, he must take a back seat, he's not a well man but I can understand why he gets so involved," he said and both Fin and I agreed.

Luiza interjected. "He's not going back to work anymore, he has to look after his health now and you two boys will have to take responsibility, take Francisco on permanently if you need him. Emil is out of the game completely, Eugene." The last comment being aimed directly to me I found a little strange but didn't give it too much thought. Dr Johnson added, "We can put him on a rehabilitation programme, sometimes the memory comes back on its own naturally but it wouldn't do any harm having a little help." Luiza nodded her agreement. "We'll take good care of him, Mrs Janowitz, don't you worry about that." he ended.

***

I was confused. I couldn't understand why the woman had said what she had. She'd told me she loved me because I was her husband of fifty years? I stood up, wanting to go to the toilet and a nurse came over to assist. "I'm ok, thanks," I told her but she took my arm anyway to support me on the way. At the wash basin, I looked in the mirror, an old man glared back and it frightened me somewhat. "Nurse!" I shouted. She came in to assist.

"How old am I?" I questioned.

"Well Mr Janowitz, I'd say you're a healthy young seventy something," she said, guessing.

"Seriously, how old am I?" I asked.

"Let's take a look at your record sheet," she said as we returned to the bed. She took a clipboard from the end and read out my age.

"Jesus! Where did all that time go?" I exclaimed.

"You've just got a little memory loss, but it'll come back to you," the nurse said.

"So is that lady really my wife?"

"Luiza, yes. You're a lucky man, she's lovely," she said.

"She sure is, but she's old," I replied without a thought.

"She's the same age as you, Emil," was the response.

"I guess you're right," I agreed.

"You know you have two children…"

I completed her sentence for her, "Lena and Daniel."

"That's right, Emil! See you do remember, it's coming back already," she said enthusiastically.

Over the next few weeks, things started returning. One day, Luiza came in with a coffee from McDuff's bar, the cup had the name on it and something connected in my memory. I remembered her face peering round a door as Eugene, Fin and I were talking. I recalled the conversation we had clearly. I looked at her as the event came flooding back. "Luiza, I remember, sweetheart, I remember!"

I held her hand as she began to cry. "Don't cry lovely, just think of all the things we'll remember together, it will be like doing it all over again," I told her.

Later that night, she entered the room with a surprise for me. "I got permission to bring him," she said as Max trotted excitedly into the room. "Max! Where's my beautiful boy, come here fella!" It was marvellous seeing my boy again, I hadn't known I'd missed him so much until that moment and instantly recalled our good times together. He couldn't stop enthusiastically licking my face, his excitement getting the better of him. I suppose to him I'd been away a lifetime.

The boys went quietly about their work and I don't recall when or what caused it, but at some point I remembered what we did. It may have been a dream or possibly a nightmare I'd had about my time in Auschwitz, I don't know exactly but I recalled how important our work was. I knew Luiza wouldn't want me to revisit it but I needed to know how they were getting on.

I asked Eugene, who I thought would be the more amenable of the two, but he rebuked my approach.

"You're not supposed to be getting involved with any of this," he cautioned.

"Just let me know where you're up to, entertain me, it'll keep my mind occupied. I promise not to get involved," I'd said half-heartedly.

"Before your stroke we had a deal to make with someone you know, a guy called Liebermann."

"Yasiel Liebermann," I interrupted.

"You remember, that's good, Emil," he commented.

"Looks like it. Yes, I remember him from Auschwitz, the son of a bitch got away didn't he, Eugene?"

"Here's the rub of it. Emil. Clearly we had to abandon that deal because he'd instructed you to pick up documentation at a bookstore at Auschwitz, a deal which would have let him go free and unpunished for what he did but in return he was going to hand Hugo Drexler on a plate to us."

"Drexler? That's who we're working on isn't it, he got away, didn't he?"

"That's right, Emil. Liebermann wouldn't trust Fin and me to do a deal."

"Jacob Altman! I'm starting to recall this Eugene, Jacob Altman, he's a friend right?" I questioned.

"He is, Emil. Jacob and I have been trying to work on Liebermann for several weeks now without any luck. He says he'll only deal with you. For some reason, he trusts you; that's what he says anyway," Eugene told me, then continued, "I've told you too much, Emil. Luiza will be angrier than a wet hen, now settle down and rest a while. Fin, Jacob and I have got this covered and with your permission we'd like to employ Francisco," he asked.

"Francisco, sure he's a good kid, he's the one with the photographic memory isn't he?"

"That's right. He was of use to us, especially in Sao Paulo," he said.

"Ok, Eugene, you've got my head spinning. Sao Paulo, I think I've got that one as well."

Months passed by and I slowly returned back to my normal self, I'd regained a lot of memory but I did the rehabilitation programme which helped, it gave me back the ability to think naturally and made me a little more confident about myself, how I went about things on a daily basis. I'd had a stroke and the prognosis had come back a lot better than was originally thought. I recovered well but had to go through a little brain retraining. Luiza set a routine for me at home, a sequence of events I'd do on a daily basis which would help my way back into the world. Slowly, I ground her down. "I need to be involved, Luiza, I'm a grown man, I know I was overdoing it but I've learned how to manage myself a lot better now. I promise I'll just oversee things, nothing too strenuous," I said, multiple times, until finally she agreed to allow me back with one condition added, she'd sit alongside me.

Like the routines she'd set in place, we sat around my desk in the study going through papers on a daily basis, the boys had gotten used to doing a report for me to analyse and give an opinion. There wasn't much to check in the beginning, but we were working together as a team once more, it was just my role had changed and I knew it had to, after all my wife was only looking after my welfare.

"Liebermann's still refusing any deals," Eugene told me. "I can't persuade him you had a stroke, he says we're playing games and he won't risk it. I've tried getting Kleinman to chase his IP address down, the last contact he had with us claimed to be from Manchester, England, but I doubt he was ever there and if he ever was he's likely somewhere else now. It looks like he's using some kind of device which camouflages his location on the 'net'. It's clever, Emil, but not unbreakable, so Kleinman says."

"Wouldn't it be easier if I just agreed to his demands? I want Liebermann more than any one of you and I've good reason to want him but I can see the greater good in this deal. We all want Drexler and all I'd have to do is go to Auschwitz," I said as Luiza grabbed my arm.

"No, Emil! You promised, you'll get worked up and have another stroke and this time it will kill you, you can't do that to your family," she countered.

"I wore you down the last time Luiza but I'm not going to do that this time, it's not fair, so I'll say this and I'll say it only once, if you come with me to Auschwitz and stand by my side with Eugene, Fin and Francisco, I promise if anything happens, I'll walk away and leave it for the boys to sort out. You and I will go take some lunch in that fancy restaurant we went to," I looked into her eyes. "Luiza, I promise you."

She looked at the boys individually knowing they needed me. "You must promise he'll not get involved in anything that will cause him any stress." They agreed. "Then we'll go, but I'm going to be so close to you Emil Janowitz that you won't be able to go to the toilet on your own," she said with conviction.

"You wouldn't think this lady was my wife would you boys, more a jailer, but she has a good heart. She thinks of me all the time and I don't deserve that love and attention. All I can say is I must be a hell of a lover, I can't remember though," I said, jokingly.

"I've got my eye on you, Mister," she replied, pointing a finger at me with suspicious eyes. I was definitely back.

Chapter 13

Raguel the Angel of Justice

The flight went well, I'd taken my medication before boarding and Luiza stuck by my side, as she said she would.

After we arrived at the hotel and settled in, I arranged a meeting in the lobby with the boys. "Remember, Emil, you're just here for the ride, you don't get too involved and you stay calm," Eugene reminded.

"I know, but I want to reaffirm what I should know and compare notes on what we've unearthed, gentlemen, just so I'm fully equipped with all of the intelligence we've gathered," I told them.

We sat round a table, drinking coffee, and went through what we'd gathered over the last many months. I kicked the session off with "I'll summarize our situation as briefly as I can, please jump in at any point with relevant information. You two discovered documents in Ilse Gerver's loft that we've categorised as the Belsen Files. By cross-referencing them with the files we already hold and those from Kaspar Stahnke's computer, we identified the former SS officer Hugo Drexler, a hitherto unknown who had some interesting connections. The former nurse at Belsen when it was liberated, Sarah Davies, identified Drexler as present within Belsen along with another man, Tauber – we know this man as Héctor Tauber. Stahnke, when he was alive, was keen to interest us in something he called 'The Lazarus Project'. We ignored him but since then we have evidence that this project actually existed. What its final purpose was we don't exactly know, it could have been intended for the reincarnation, or cloning, of people considered essential to the Nazi cause in the future or it could have been connected to the 'purity of race' programmes, intended to genetically produce a superior racial type. We don't exactly know. Have I got that right so far?"

Fin and Eugene nodded and allowed me to continue. "Ok, We did have an idea of tracing the huge amounts of funds the Nazis looted from Holocaust locations, including Croatia, as indicated in one of Stahnke's digital files but, as we know, after many discussions we had to accept that was an impossible task for us, greater powers appeared to have failed or *probably* just ignored the issue because it suited their post war aims. We *had* to concentrate on something we could achieve and for a while there was a conflict of interests between you two; Bormann or Drexler. We chose Drexler because the more Mr Quinn here delved into it the more it looked as if the German reports and confirmations of his death were in fact true. There were some anomalies there but strangely they brought us back to the Lazarus Project and to Drexler, who we believe inadvertently helped fuel sightings in South America of Hitler's personal secretary by using an alias that Simon Wiesenthal had wrongly attributed to Bormann."

I paused to see if they wanted to correct me, but they didn't so I carried on. "We found that 'Disciples' list as well. Of those listed, their career backgrounds in the programmes of murderous elimination strongly suggested that their mission, should they have survived the war, was to carry on 'Lazarus' with an ultimate goal of enabling the rise of a Fourth Reich. Let's face it *'they'* still have the funds somewhere. We now know the Nazis were carrying out DNA research with a view to manipulation. They'd gathered samples from their finest people and their best 'warriors'. Throughout this, our inquiries kept leading back to the man that even the Wiesenthal Center had never heard of – Hugo Drexler, who we know was the man chosen to lead the Lazarus Project; the man who can tell us, finally, what the purpose of it was and why all those innocent people had to die to achieve it. Now, we could go into detail, boys, but I don't think at this moment it would do *me* any good. Have I got a reasonable grip on where we came from and where we've arrived?"

Eugene looked at Findlay. They were in agreement. "That's about it, Emil," Eugene said. "Drexler's our prize. If we can find him alive and bring him to justice, he'll be the most important hidden Nazi we've ever apprehended. But, are you still willing to lose Liebermann?"

I couldn't help a regretful smile. "Losing Yasiel Liebermann is a price I'm willing to pay for the head of Drexler. It's a god damn shame we can't deliver both men into the hands of justice, but in order to move forward, a compromise *has* to be made."

***

Altman called me the following day. "Emil, my friend, listen carefully. You're to go to the book shop in Auschwitz 1, tomorrow between two and half past. Ask for Feliks, he's in his forties with a receding hairline. I'm told he'll give you an A4 envelope and further instructions. Be careful, my friend."

***

I'd been inside the bookstore before with Luiza, our visit back in '93, it brought to mind a need for water; the whole place left a bad taste in my mouth. We arrived in a taxi, the 'boys' shadowing in a hired car. They parked up and kept their distance, only Luiza and I walked in.

"Excuse me, do you speak English?" I enquired at the counter.

"I speak English, Mr Janowitz," came a reply from behind. I turned to see the man who'd been described to me the previous day.

"My name is Feliks. I'm Herr Liebermann's representative in this matter." He extended his arm towards the exit door. "Please, come with me, I have something to give to you."

Once outside, I asked him, "Do you have the envelope?"

"Patience, Mr Janowitz. First, I have instructions to accompany you to Block 10, the directive is quite clear, I'm not to hand over a thing until then."

Why would he want me to set eyes on block 10 once more? I'd seen it enough times and had hoped I'd never see it ever again.

"What is it you need me to see there?" I persisted.

"I only know to take you there and nothing more," he replied and beckoned us to follow him.

Then I remembered I was with Luiza, she shot me a cautionary glance; I shrugged and took her hand.

"You were a prisoner here weren't you, Mr Janowitz," Feliks said as we walked. "I don't think I could start to imagine the memories you have of this place."

I said nothing but had an unpleasant, sinking feeling in the pit of my stomach, more than that though, it made me feel light headed, dizzy, the air became humid and hard to breathe, my legs felt weak and wobbly. Luiza was right on it. "Feliks wait!" she called out. "Fetch some water, my husband isn't a well man, he shouldn't be doing this!" she barked at him before turning to me. "You need to sit down for a moment, Emil. Here, can you make it to that bench?"

"Yes, but I'm alright Luiza, it's this place, no man should return to the site of their family's death. Things happened here you couldn't possibly imagine, it's hard," I said, shaking my head from side to side, trying to overcome the feeling of emotion that was devouring me.

Feliks returned and proffered a small bottle of mineral water. "I'm sorry, Mr Janowitz, I didn't know any of this, I was simply given a job to do," he told us.

I sat for several minutes and drank half the water whilst eating a chocolate bar Luiza took from her bag.

"Let's carry on, Feliks," I said, when I'd finished. "I have to get that envelope. I feel better now."

"You *must* tell me if it gets too much for you, Emil Janowitz," Luiza scolded.

"Yes, I will," I confirmed and held out a hand for comfort, her's more so than mine.

Within minutes, we were presented with the five steps that would take us to the flat concrete area in front of a rusty colored heavy door. A lamp, decorated with a blackened metal number '10', was fixed to the wall and next to this was a wooden panel inscribed '10 Block'. Now I knew why Liebermann wanted me at *this* building. Just the sight of it filled me with fear and yet I had to fight it, I had to go inside once more.

The door opened inwardly, exposing a long corridor, one I remembered vividly. Ayla and Bina Goshen, the twin girls who revisited my memory like ghosts, had walked this corridor, like so many others. I never did find out what became of them. I saw their faces in detail and curiously remembered their long blonde hair I'd witnessed upon their entry to the camp.

Feliks interrupted my thoughts. "This way, Mr Janowitz."

"I've been here before," I said, my voice faltering as I turned to my wife. "I know this place."

"I know you do, sweetheart, I know," she replied, placing her hand on my arm to soothe me. "We'll get out of here as fast as we can," she said.

"No, I don't mean just that. This corridor means something more. I've walked down here. This is the dream, it's where I saw my family when I had the seizure, I told you I saw my family didn't I? It was here." Why was it here? Of all the places, why here?"

"Emil, let's get this over with, sweetheart. This place is starting to frighten me," she whispered.

Tears were forming in my eyes but I had to get the letter, no matter how hard it became. I pressed on.

"In here, Mr Janowitz," Feliks pointed to a room, it was a room where many Nazi doctors had conducted twisted experiments: Mengele, Clauberg, Schumann, Wirths, Weber and Hirst had all used this place.

A shadow of my past appeared to my right hand side and suddenly I was seeing faces I knew; they crept inside my soul from out of nowhere, people I'd not thought of in over fifty years. Olaf Bal, Mateusz Zubek, Albin Drozda, all murdered by Mengele in this room, it was like they'd been waiting all these years for my return. Fabian Rusak, Bolesław Kapala, Anatol Klepacki, the names kept coming, their faces too. So many innocent people butchered by a cabal of murderers.

Feliks went to a work cabinet fixed to the wall, it was old, definitely an original; those who visited this place so many years later could not adequately imagine the horror and terror it would have witnessed but I'd read somewhere *'knowledge is sorrow, they who know the most must mourn the deepest over the fatal truth'* – and I knew.

He reached into one of its drawers and retrieved an A4 envelope. Then, he placed a key on the worktop that I'd not noticed him use, so preoccupied had I been by my thoughts. He handed the letter over and I opened it. It was a legal document, written in English with a copy attached.

"Read it, Mr Janowitz, then when you are satisfied, please sign it," Feliks said.

I did as he requested. In long winded legalese it basically stated that no one knowing and/or employed or associated in any manner with Emil Janowitz and/or the late Aleksy Markowski could use any information whatsoever contained within any of their files, whether they be digital renditions, originals or copies in any form, or such files of others, which referred to the Holocaust and/or any matter connected with the running of any camp within the Nazi camp system, in the prosecution of Liebermann.

With a heavy heart, I accepted the pen Feliks offered, put the master document on the worktop and signed it. I couldn't allow Hugo Drexler to walk away from justice. Feliks received the papers and handed me a small envelope. "You can open now if you wish, or perhaps later." Then he added, "But, if I were you, I would do it now."

Within, I found a folded piece of paper upon which was written – Av Pedroso de Morais, 2293, Alto de Pinheiros, São Paulo, Brazil. Leandro Medina is Hugo Drexler.

He stepped out of the room and beckoned us to follow. In the corridor, he told us, "Thank you for your cooperation in this matter, Mr Janowitz, Mrs Janowitz. I must leave you now but you can see the entrance we came in, straight down the corridor. Your colleagues, I am told, have slipped into the last room on your right and I'm sure they will open the door for you, I suspect it may be too heavy for you or your wife."

He gave us a formal nod of his head which is when I realised what I had taken to be a very discreet hearing aid, wasn't. He turned and walked away.

Sure enough, as we were almost at the door, Eugene and Findlay slipped from the shadows.

"How'd it go, Emil?" Eugene said, quietly.

I handed him the envelope with the note in it and we left the building. I never wanted to return to this place again.

That night, I had a fitful sleep, the little bird came to me and I heard a voice say:

'His name is Raguel; archangel of justice, one of seven and his number is six. He is Raguel the Watcher, one who will sit in judgement then bring redemption or retribution. I have seen his work and it is both wondrous and terrifying to behold.'

Chapter 14

Leandro Medina

Luiza forbid Emil from taking any further active part in the investigation. He protested, of course, but to no avail, we supported her fully, the forces of good were too much for him.

We did our homework. The building occupying Av Pedroso de Morais, 2293, in the São Paulo suburb of Alto de Pinheiros was an unobtrusive place, listed as a private hospital. Posing as a relative, Fin was able to confirm that Leandro Medina was, indeed, a patient.

We stepped off the plane, passed through passport control and were met by Francisco in the hire car. He took us direct to our destination.

Arriving at the address Yasiel Liebermann exchanged for his liberty, we wandered up to the reception desk.

"We're here to pay a visit to a gentleman by the name of Leandro Medina," Fin told the attractive receptionist.

"And who are you?" she enquired, pleasantly.

Fin showed her the false ID he'd had produced by a shady contact of his and told her, "I'm Bruno Medina. Leandro is a relative of mine."

She queried that. "We were told he had no relatives?"

Fin smiled, sweetly. "Not in Brazil, but me and Ma, back in New York, are the last as far as we know. He's my great uncle, but when she heard from an old friend he wasn't very well, seeing as I would be here on business, Ma was insistent that I should come and see him. You know what mothers are like."

She did but asked who I was. Fin replied, "This guy? He's my buddy, Harry, he had nothing better to do so thought he'd give me some moral support." We were directed to the ward, after she'd made a phone call.

At the entrance, a large woman with short dark hair walked towards us. There were more questions then she said, "Please sign your names here," pointing her finger to a line on the clipboard she produced from the nurses' station. Having passed inspection, we were led to a place they called the 'Day Room'.

"Mr Medina has an illness they call Fibromyalgia," she said. "It's a disorder that causes him widespread musculoskeletal pain and as a result he suffers from fatigue, poor memory and mood swings. It has been complicated by the discovery of an inoperable cancerous brain tumour. He struggles with events that took place in the past other than vague recollections. Often, he doesn't even respond to his name." I could understand that, he probably hadn't had enough time to commit it to full memory. I just hoped he'd remember who he really was.

The sole occupant of the room was a grey haired, well-presented old man dressed in beige slacks, white short sleeved shirt with a black tie. He was looking out into the garden. As we stood before him, I noticed his shoes were patent leather and the emblem of the Thule society was sewn into the tie. Now, aware of our presence, he turned to examine us. It was Drexler alright.

We pulled up a couple of chairs and sat next to him. I smiled and said, "Hello, Mr Drexler. My name is Eugene Kennedy and this is Findlay Quinn. We want to ask you a few questions."

"Why do you call me Drexler," he replied, firmly.

"It's the name you were born under, Mr Drexler. Can I call you Hugo?"

"No, you cannot." He looked like he was going to say something else and his finger quivered over his lips.

Fin told him, "We know who you are, Drexler."

He sat and stared back at us for a few moments then finally said, "Do you know my brother? He was a lot older than me but passed away some years ago."

I responded, "Yeah, we knew of your brother, a great man but you were greater."

"Yes, he could have been but he was a drunk you know. He always thought he was better than me but I proved him wrong."

I gave him my best friendly smile. "You certainly did. He never got his name on 'die Jüngerliste' and he never got chosen to head up 'das Lazarus Projekt'.

"You know about this?"

"Yes, we know but what was the purpose of the 'Disciples', why so many?"

It sounded like he was already back in time, in his head, which suited us fine; neither of us wanted him to return to the here and now.

He smiled. "We were the most dedicated to the cause. Not to Hitler, though he definitely thought so, but the cause of National Socialism. It was my idea, 'the Disciples'. Hitler loved it, he thought he was a new Christ, you know. That's why I picked that particular name."

"What was your purpose?"

He looked at me as if I was simple minded. "Why, to keep the cause alive, to bring the world a pure race, a race that was fit to rule."

"Yes of course, but why so many?" I tried again.

"It was to be a safeguard, should anything happen to any of us. We had the funding, you know, hidden away; Himmler had arranged it, him and Speer."

"And Lazarus?" I pressed him.

He waved a finger at us. "Ahh, Lazarus. What a glorious project. What great science. We were leaps and bounds ahead of everyone for so long, decades in fact, but it was hard to keep up the momentum. That fool, Eichmann, getting himself caught caused the problems, before that everything was fine. Bloody Jews! They were only streets away from me! Mengele nearly filled his pants. We were in the process of negotiating with the Argentines for a purpose built pharmaceutical facility. Do you know the cost of such a place? A lot less than all the bribes we had to pay. All ruined by Eichmann, and we lost that money. Things got more difficult after that, Mengele wanted to do his own thing and we quarrelled. We never spoke for years but we'd remade contact and he came to my laboratory, in the hills, outside Bertioga. Then, the bloody fool managed to drown, sunning himself at the beach."

Suddenly, he looked as us strangely. "Who did you say you were? Why have you come here?"

Fin stepped in. "We wanted to discuss your work. You know, 'gene variants' and 'risk variants' that sort of thing. How close were you to cloning?"

It seemed to relapse him. "Cloning? Oh, we were close, so very close but what does it matter. The British beat us to it, beat *me* to it. I couldn't find where I'd gone wrong and my illness was becoming too much. I had to forget all that and find what I could do about the pain. Risk variants, yes, that's what I had to find, what was wrong with my own genes to cause this pain. I had to isolate the gene, you see, and modify it, find out how to eradicate the defect." Something in his eyes suddenly changed. "But, why are you asking me all this? I've already told you people, you have my research and you can see all the work I did. In centuries to come, I will be lauded as a person of extreme importance in science."

Fin and I exchanged concerned glances. "Who have you already told, Hugo?" Fin asked.

He began to get angry. "Your people! Your people! You're idiots! Why am I always surrounded by idiots?!"

He lunged at me, trying to slap my face. Fin gripped him, talking soothingly, placing him back in his chair. Unfortunately, the noise had attracted attention and a doctor came in and asked us to step outside, leaving him with a nurse.

"Gentlemen, I don't know why you are here, but Mr Medina is not a well man. His brain cancer is advancing rapidly. I'm afraid I cannot allow you to continue your visit."

That was it, so it seemed. We'd gotten some answers but possibly not the ones we'd wanted. We'd started with the idea of a huge conspiracy and the possibility of a concerted effort to reincarnate top Nazi leaders, create a pure race and invigorate a new Reich, a Fourth Reich, and found that what we had was yet another Nazi dream that had gone the way of the others and collapsed. We walked into the corridor outside the ward and were approached by two suits.

"Gentlemen, please step in this office, it's a matter of national security," the lead guy said, flashing some ID. Door closed, he told us to sit down so we occupied the only two seats there were.

"Mr Quinn, Mr Kennedy. We represent the Government of the United States. I know you've probably put a lot of work into getting this far but you're involvement in this matter is now ended. Do I make myself clear?"

Fin couldn't help let a little smile escape. "It would be clearer if you told us the truth. Let's see the ID properly; you sure as hell ain't State Department."

Lead man looked at his partner who was casually resting his butt against the radiator by the window then brought out the ID again, allowing Fin to scrutinise it.

"So, you're CIA, see how easy that was. Now, what's your problem with what we're doing?"

"It's a national security matter. Drexler's under the protection of the Agency, for the time being."

"And when will he not be under your protection?" I chipped in.

"When he's dead."

Fin eyed him up through a squint then said, "It's not him your interested in, not anymore, is it? I take it you've got all his research papers?"

Lead man glanced at his partner again who released a hardly discernible nod, but it wasn't so much agreement as permission. That's when we knew we weren't talking to the organ grinder.

Fin turned to the other guy. "How about *you* just tell us? You're clearly the string puller in this team."

The room fell silent. Radiator guy looked down at the floor, stroked his forehead between thumb and forefinger and let out a hint of a sigh.

"Guys, I know you've probably put a lot of work into this. A lot of time, sweat and tears, no doubt. But, here's the thing. Mr Drexler, in there, was well ahead of his time. Cloning, gene research and modification, dare I say gene perfection. That he didn't succeed doesn't mean that his research isn't of great interest to science. I *could* tell you it's of great interest to your Government but at the moment it isn't. It is, however, of huge interest to the Agency and DARPA."

Fin caught my quizzical look. "Defense Advanced Research Projects Agency, Eugene."

Radiator man nodded his thanks and continued. "We were sent to get you to peacefully go back home and forget everything but something about the pair of you tells me that'll only piss you off so I'm going to offer you a deal.

"If you don't take it, you won't make it to the airport before you get busted for drugs. You'll be in a Brazilian jail for weeks, if not months, before it gets quietly brushed under the carpet. Now, I know what you'll be thinking. You'll go to the Press but I have to tell you that our assets in *all* the mainstream media will kill it dead. They won't touch you. You might make page four in the Pigshit, Wyoming, Herald but that's as far as it'll get. So, here's the offer.

"You can take Drexler to court but I think we all know, because of his condition and prognosis, he's never going to stand trial. In any event, his lawyers will spin the proceedings out for as long as it takes. I can guarantee you this man isn't going to be here long. Heck, he'll most probably be dead inside two months, if not before. In return for the opportunity to complete your job you have to agree *not* to refer to Drexler's research, personal or otherwise and *not* to mention or allude to the Lazarus Project. If you do mention or try to use any of it in Court or in the Press, you'll find yourselves *and* your boss in a world of shit you could never imagine. I dare say, it's very possible it might kill him, given his health problems at the moment."

"Jeez, that's a very tempting offer." Fin responded, sarcastically. "What do you think, Gene?"

They all looked at me. I was thinking hard, my mind speeding through possibilities then I found myself saying, "Can I just speak to my colleague in private?"

Radiator man nodded. "You've got one minute" and his partner followed him out.

"Fin," I said, urgently. "I think what he's saying is that if we don't indict on the basis of the genetics research and Lazarus but on the basis of Drexler's overall responsibility for the Nazi department that oversaw the experiments by the SS doctors in the camps, then despite our chances of success being zero, and you know it as well as I do, the publicity generated will send out a very clear message that no matter how old they are, they *will* be found and denounced. As long as we do as he says and don't breach the national security issues we'll have achieved our aim."

"Did he actually say that, Gene?"

"No, but he alluded to it by not mentioning it in the list of forbidden things."

"I don't know, Gene, but I can't think of a better solution. I'm pretty sure I can survive a Brazilian jail intact but I'm worried about you, 'pretty boy'. I doubt you'd get even one decent shower unmolested. Ok, we'll take it."

I tapped the door and they came back in. "So, what you mean is that as long as the research and Lazarus are not mentioned we can indict on him having had overall responsibility for the experimentation in the camps?"

"Correct, Mr Kennedy. We have a deal?"

"Yes, we have a deal. What are you going to do with all his research?"

Radiator man considered the matter, the matter of whether to tell us anything at all, then said, "We'll be doing something a bit more interesting than shoving it in a cupboard or under the bed which is all you could have done with it, Mr Kennedy. *Those* people are dead and I for one don't think they should have died in vain, so I'm good with it."

We spent the night at Francisco's place, a few consolation beers. It wasn't easy breaking the news to him but in the end he saw we'd gotten the best result possible in the circumstances. Emil was expecting an update. I wanted to toss a coin for who would do it but Fin took Francisco by the arm and told him they were going for a beer at the bar across the street. I popped another beer from the fridge and drank half of it before

I had the courage to make the call. I sure as hell wasn't going to tell Emil the truth, not just now. I didn't want to raise his blood pressure. I told him we had to go back the next day and things were going well then I joined the guys in the bar.

Before we had to make the airport, we had sufficient time to return to the hospital and speak to the doctor from the previous day. He wasn't of a mind to cooperate until we told him straight what responsibility his patient had in the deaths of so many people. When we reminded him that those responsible were all doctors, he told us he felt disgusted that such people existed. He said, "The oath I took included the words 'I will utterly reject harm and mischief' and 'I will remember that I do not treat a fever chart, a cancerous growth, but a sick human being'. When I teach juniors about how to help patients I remind them these are not blood tests – they are people. You realise it is my duty to give this man the best that I can. Some may hate him but he is my patient. In which case, I do not believe I am breaking the vow to respect secrets confided in me when I give you my report on his illnesses, treatment and prognosis. However, truly this man will not be going to heaven."

It wasn't easy breaking the news to Emil but once he'd read the doctors report he conceded we'd done the right thing. All we had to do was get the evidence ready for the Grand Jury. We worked around the clock, got a general session's court date and moved on through. Emil reckoned it could take 2 to 5 months to get to the Grand Jury but we made it in just under three. We'd expected to hear news every day that Drexler died but each time we checked in with his doctors for some reason he was still in this world.

We got the indictment, we got the publicity, lots of it and then we got the news that he was dead. We'd been riding on a sort of adrenalin high, Luiza helping out and keeping Emil at arm's length from the activity for his own good but when the news came, it came as a kinda relief to us all. We honestly didn't know how long we could have kept it up before we burnt out. I went home to Jody that evening for a quiet meal and a hunker down on the couch watching romantic comedies, back to back. I knew I needed it to soothe my soul, and hers;

she'd had a lot to put up with. The next day, I found out from Fin he went out with some friends and got blind drunk. Emil went to bed early with Luiza, a good book and a cup of hot chocolate, Max at the foot of the bed.

*****

Later that week Fin called, he had something he wanted to talk to me about, something he had to do face to face he said.

We met at Macduff's Bar' in Greenwich. I sat wondering what it could be that was so urgent then he walked in and gesticulated if I wanted a beer. I gave him the thumbs up and waited for him to sit down.

"Eugene" he hesitated, somewhat nervously, "You were adopted as a child weren't you," he announced.

"No, Fin. I wasn't. What's this about," I enquired, uneasily.

He took a big swig of his beer and said, "I don't know how to say this so I'm just going to come out and say it. I was intrigued by the photograph I found a few months back of Emil, one that had a resemblance of you. I mentioned it to you but I didn't show you it did I?"

"No," I replied, enquiringly.

"Here, take a look." The print was a little dog eared. As I examined it, I could see a young man that had Emil's looks about him, then stood next to him I noticed the image of myself. "Wow, a doppelgänger. They do say everyone's got one," I declared, nervously laughing.

"It's more than that, Gene. I did a little more digging, in some ways I wish I hadn't because I don't know if you'll value what I found but I can assure you I did it in good faith," he said anxiously.

"What the hell have you found?" I said.

"First of all, I want you to know Emil's a good man. He's watched over you since he found out who you are."

"*Who I am?*" I questioned with a raised voice.

Fin finished his beer, got up and went to the bar, leaving me staring at myself in the photo.

Coming back with two fresh drinks, he sat down and said, "There's no easy way of saying this, your real father died at Auschwitz, Gene. His name was Filip."

I interrupted, "My father lives in Queens, Fin, with my mother."

"I know that, Gene, and they're good people," then it all came out in one big chunk, "but your real father was Emil's brother, Filip. You were conceived in the Warsaw Ghetto, your father knew nothing of your mother's pregnancy, she escaped through the Polish resistance and was hidden by the Catholic Church, she died of typhus shortly after and you were included in a shipment of orphaned children sanctioned by the Red Cross to come to America during the latter days of the war. You were then sent to the Zion of Jerusalem Orphanage in New York were you were adopted at three years of age by the childless Kennedy family, who it seems never mentioned you were adopted. I guess, they wanted you to have a normal childhood and not be burdened by what you'd been through. I don't know why I'm telling you this but I think it may explain why Emil calls you Filip and why he looks at you like a son, clearly he cares a lot for you. Gene, the man's been to hell and back and then found out his only brother had a son. He decided to look after you the best way he could. He didn't interfere with the life you had with your parents, he knew they loved you just as much as he did, he's not a selfish man, he's the least selfish man I know. Emil's your uncle," he said.

I searched his face for any hint this was somehow an elaborate and not very kind joke but all I saw was discomfort and I knew he was telling the truth. Without warning, tears ran down my cheeks. I wiped them and cupped my face. "Jesus, it's true, isn't it? I knew there was something odd about it all but I wouldn't have ever guessed this though." I clutched the photograph of my father in my hands, staring at it. "Why tell me now, Fin?"

"Gene, I've known for some weeks. I didn't want to tell you to begin with but things started developing with Emil, his age and the deterioration of his memory, sooner or later he'd have permanently seen you as his brother and I thought it only fair to tell you why. You'd have become Filip to him. A year, who knows, maybe even five but I'm sure it's going to happen. He's getting more and more muddled around you lately."

I tried to stand up but my legs gave way a little. Fin grabbed me and held me firm. "That's some news, Fin," I said, whilst trying to compose myself.

Later that day in Idar Court, I took a purposeful look at Emil. Whilst staring at him, I caught myself deliberating on whether I should say anything and he noticed.

"Is there something wrong, Eugene?"

"No, I'm fine. I just want to thank you for everything you've done for me, you're a good man."

"Thank me for what, Eugene? You do a damn good job, despite my being a pain in the ass to be around and paying you less than you deserve," he joked.

"No, Emil, *you* are a good man and a good friend too. I sat down at my computer, pondering how I'd actually gotten this job in the first place, recollecting I'd picked up a copy of the New York Times from the desk sergeant at the NYPD whilst waiting on paperwork to be filed for a felony. The page was already open and the job highlighted on the advert headed 'Detective wanted to work on historical files'. I was now starting to suspect that a certain old, retired detective might have placed the newspaper there moments earlier.

The old man must have been watching my back for years. He'd headed up the Fletcher child killer case before he retired and I'd become involved in that, through a lucky arrest. He must have seen me somewhere, probably the courthouse waiting to give evidence and spotted the resemblance even back then. He looked over towards me with curiosity.

"You sure you're alright, Eugene? Can I get you a tea or a sandwich or something?" he said, smiling at me with that familiar friendly face. I smiled back trying hard not to say what I wanted to. "No, I'm fine, honestly. I've just had some news that's all."

"Is Jody okay, take some time off if you need to, this work can wait, your home life is more important," he replied with emphasis.

"Emil, really, I'm okay," I responded and smiled again but this time with feeling. He was my uncle and I knew how much he loved Filip, he'd told me often enough. I knew now why I'd been dreaming the way I had, something in the ether of life was pushing me forward, helping me to find justice for my father.

As I was staring at the monitor in a world of my own, I thought about Filip, what he'd been through and the dreadful way he'd died. I wished I could have met him.

Emil always told me he was '*a good boy*', he always saw him that way, never imagining the man he could have grown to be. I thought about how upset my real parents might be if they found out that I knew about the adoption and decided there and then to never tell them, it would hurt them too much and they didn't deserve that, they were both good people. I'd keep what Fin had told me to myself, though I was undecided about Emil. It was a decision I couldn't quite make at that point of time, it was too soon.

The screen went blank which jolted me from deep thought. I turned to see Emil looking directly at me, "Something *is* wrong, you can tell me, I'm a good listener. A problem shared so they say and I think a lot about you, you're a good boy," he said in familiar tones. "I'd do anything for you if needed," he added.

"I know you would, Emil, and I appreciate it, thanks, it means a lot. I'm just feeling a little wiped out today. I think I need a beer tonight, would you like to join me?" I saw the twinkle in his eyes. "Did you hear that, Luiza? Eugene is feeling a little under the weather, he says he needs to talk to me about the case but he needs a little fresh air," he called.

She came rushing into the room, "Are you alright, Eugene?" then started fussing.

"I'm alright guys, I just need some fresh air," I said, backing Emil up.

"You'd best go with him, Emil, make sure he's okay," she said, earnestly.

Emil hastily grabbed his jacket and led me by the arm to the front door.

"You'll need this," Luiza held his wallet out in front of her."

"Ah yes. I think we need milk," he replied.

"Go on, scram the pair of you, you think old Luiza's head buttons up at the back. Don't be late," she said, grabbing Emil by the ears, pulling his head downward and kissing him on the top of the head.

I walked out with a smile, they were a funny old couple. "That woman's got secondary vision, always has had," he mumbled under his breath.

Epilogue

I looked through the glass into Hugo Drexler's room as the nurses tended to him. I'd allowed him to suffer for years, tormenting him with pain for the crimes he'd committed but it was time for him to leave soon. I caught what the doctor had said and he was right, he wouldn't be going to heaven. I had other plans for him.

When he could still speak, he told them about me at the window, 'It's there! It's come for me! At the window! It's at the window!' But, they couldn't see, only he. When he was unable to communicate anymore he'd simply silently scream. To the nurses, he just lay there with his mouth open and eyes staring. They had to lubricate both for his comfort. They didn't hear him screaming, you see. I could hear him though.

I would watch him, constantly, and I could hear his call of torment and suffering. The medical staff had no idea of the anguish that enveloped him when he saw me, and he always saw me. When he finally died, they said he would be at peace but I knew he would never be at peace, not his kind. His torment and fear would be as endless as the universe.

I now had other things to do again. I'd continue to watch over an extraordinary man who, though much nearer to the end of his life than the beginning, persistently and selflessly put others before himself and did good in the world.

I was lucky, I'd chosen well and had the chance to do a good thing myself – swapping souls with him all those years ago had saved many lives but only I knew how he revealed his true identity; it was his smile.

I loved him like a brother but my time would soon pass to another, but not yet, we still had work to do.

Printed in Great Britain
by Amazon